He'd gone husbandly on her.

Griffin came up behind her at the sink, moved her hair to one side and kissed the back of her neck.

It was part of Griffin's nature, something that was deeply ingrained in him. She doubted he could change it, no matter how hard he tried.

Did that mean she couldn't change her wifely nature, either?

She turned to face him and their eyes met. Neither said anything, which only made the moment more intense. She wanted to put her head on his shoulder, to hold him, to never let him go.

Fear reared its anxious head. Was it possible for her to follow her friend Zoe's footsteps, to fall madly, desperately, crazily in love with Griffin the way Zoe had taken the tumble for Sean?

Yes, she thought with a jolt of panic. It was possible. But how she would survive it went beyond comprehension. They'd agreed this was only an a

Available in July 2009
from Mills & Boon® Intrigue

Killer Passion

SHERI WHITEFEATHER

MILLS & BOON®

Pure reading pleasure™

All the characters in this book have no existence outside the
imagination of the author, and have no relation whatsoever to anyone
bearing the same name or names. They are not even distantly inspired
by any individual known or unknown to the author, and all the
incidents are pure invention.

First published in Great Britain 2009
by Harlequin Mills & Boon Limited,
Eton House, 18-24 Paradise Road, Richmond, Surrey TW9 1SR

© Sheree Henry-WhiteFeather 2008

ISBN: 978 0 263 87307 8

46-0709

Harlequin Mills & Boon policy is to use papers that are
natural, renewable and recyclable products and made from
wood grown in sustainable forests. The logging and
manufacturing processes conform to the legal environmental
regulations of the country of origin.

Printed and bound in Spain
by Litografia Rosés S.A., Barcelona

ABOUT THE AUTHOR

Sheri WhiteFeather pens a variety of romances and has earned several prestigious readers' and reviewers' choice awards. She has become known for incorporating Native American elements into her stories. Her husband and children are tribally enrolled members of the Muscogee Creek Nation.

Sheri's hobbies include decorating with antiques and shopping in thrift stores for vintage clothes. Currently, she lives in a cowboy community in Central Valley, California. She loves to hear from her readers. To contact Sheri, visit her website at www.SheriWhiteFeather.com.

To Nina Bruhns and Cindy Dees
for the fictional fun in Fiji.

Chapter 1

*K*eep going, Alicia Greco told herself. *Keep running. Imagine that someone is chasing you. That he's closing in, that your life depends on this.*

Yeah, right. Her life depended on jogging on a beach in Fiji. She would've laughed if she weren't so damn winded, if she weren't struggling to put one foot in front of the other, if her calves didn't ache.

She hated to exercise, *hated* it, but she was pushing thirty and determined to stay in shape. To her, there was nothing sexier than a runner's body with all those long, lean, toned muscles.

She glanced around, focusing on the beauty of her break-of-dawn surroundings. The sun rose above the cliffs, sprinkling the ground with warm, rich hues. The ocean rolled upon the shore, the water crystal clear and breathtakingly blue. Thatch-roofed cabanas decorated the sand.

Alicia was the only person around. Other hotel guests had stirred, but they weren't making use of the beach. Before she'd set out for her run, an early-bird group of travelers had boarded a bus destined for a "Sunrise Island" tour. Everyone else was probably smart enough to be sleeping or lazily greeting the day.

She peered over her shoulder to see how far she'd gone. The main building of the resort had diminished in size, not so small that it looked like one of those little Monopoly game-piece hotels, but she was making progress.

Huffing along, she faced forward again, then caught a glimpse of something stirring at the edge of a nearby cabana. Fabric, she thought. An article of clothing. Giving in to her curious nature, she ran toward it to take a closer look and nearly stumbled to her hands and knees.

Oh my God…ohmyGod…ohmyGod…ohmyGod…

Inside the cabana, a naked man was slumped over a naked woman, his hips positioned between her open legs. Blood covered the base of his skull, matting his hair. Angry wounds slashed his back. Dark red smears trailed down his spine and onto his buttocks.

Alicia just stood, gazing at the horror laid out before her. Although most of the woman's body was trapped beneath her partner's bulk, her lifeless face was turned in Alicia's direction, her eyes fixed in a blank stare. A gaping hole gouged her neck.

Blood. So much blood. Like a slasher film, too gruesome to be real.

But it *was* real.

A special effects team hadn't trussed up a pair of actors. There were no lights, no cameras, no action. The female corpse staring into space with her throat slit wasn't going to wink or smile or sit up to sign autographs.

If she found celebrity, it would be from being a victim of the Sex on the Beach Killer.

This had to be his work, Alicia thought. The madman stalking South Pacific beaches for lovers to slay.

A chill sluiced through her own blood, icing her veins, making her tremble. She should turn away; she should run as fast as her feet would take her. But she didn't. Suddenly the dead woman seemed familiar. Alicia had seen her before. Last night…yes…last night at the hotel disco, dirty dancing with…

Instinctively, she moved to the other side of the cabana to see the dead man's face. It was him. The woman's erotic dance partner. Alicia had watched them grinding to rhythmic beats. She'd been captivated by their provocative display of affection. They'd been the most beautiful couple at the disco. Both tanned, both strikingly blond.

Both murdered.

Had the killer been in the nightclub, too? Had he seen them dance? Had he followed them onto the beach? Had he crouched in the dark while they'd kissed and touched and removed their clothes?

Rip. Slash.

Alicia could almost feel the killer's knife tear into her own flesh. Panicked, she put her hands to her throat, as if stemming a sticky crimson flow.

Before she screamed, fainted or vomited, she spun

away from the crime scene, and the shocking reality—
the stupidity of staring blatantly at the dead—nearly
knocked the air from her lungs.

She ran.

Away from the bloodied cabana. Away from the blond
couple who were no longer beautiful. Away from the
nightmare imprinted on her mind.

Her words came back to haunt her. *Imagine that
someone is chasing you. That he's closing in, that your
life depends on this.*

She raced across the thickness of the sand, wondering why the lovers had taken such a dangerous risk.
Didn't they know about the killer? Hadn't they heard the
media reports? Or listened to what other tourists were
saying? The don't-have-sex-on-the-beach warnings? The
keep-your-pants-zipped jokes?

Alicia reached the resort and, limbs still shaking,
jogged toward the main building.

Lush foliage flanked her way. The Siga Resort,
located on the mainland, was designed to reflect Fiji's
colorful culture while providing the ultimate in comfort
and luxury. The spacious rooms occupied two- and three-
story buildings, and garden paths linked the hotel blocks
to the restaurant and bar buildings. Golf, racquet and
yacht clubs were available by shuttle bus.

It was Alicia's job to pay close attention to every
detail, to evaluate every aspect of the property. She
worked for the Secret Traveler, a company that provided
star ratings, and she'd been sent to Fiji to rate the tropical
resort.

Finding butchered bodies on the beach wasn't
supposed to be part of the deal.

She wasn't the only Secret Traveler employee to get caught up in this. On another Fijian island, her friend and coworker, Zoë Conrad, had fallen in love with Sean Guthrie, a man who'd been wrongly accused of slaughtering a young couple who'd rented one of his yachts.

At the time, the authorities hadn't been aware that they had a serial killer in their midst, not until Zoë and Sean had pieced together the puzzle and cleared Sean of being a suspect.

Alicia entered the main building, approached the front desk and reported the bodies. Within no time, the Siga Resort morphed into a zoo.

Hotel guests and employees weren't permitted to leave the premises until further notice, creating an anxious stir. The authorities arrived, descended on the crime scene and blocked access to the beach. Alicia gave her statement to the police and waited for what came next—which happened to be the media.

They appeared in droves, taking an immediate interest in Alicia because she'd found the bodies. Camera bulbs flashed in her eyes and microphones appeared in front of her face. She started to babble, like she always did when she got nervous, stringing incoherent sentences together. A uniformed officer came to her rescue and whisked her away from the press.

Later, she was escorted to the police station to be interviewed by two different law enforcement officials: A Fijian inspector, then a special agent with the FBI.

The first interview exhausted Alicia, not because Inspector Inoke wasn't a polite or patient man, but because she couldn't relax.

The room in which she sat was small, and her knees threatened to bump the edge of the table. The bodies kept invading in her mind. What had compelled her to look so closely at them, to be that brazen with her psyche? How she was supposed to sleep tonight with bloodied images zigzagging through her brain, she didn't have a clue. Alicia already knew too much about this case. This was the fifth double homicide within the span of four months on four different island nations.

She reached for the water the inspector had given her. He'd already refilled her disposable cup twice, and now she was alone, taking yet another much-needed sip while waiting for the federal agent.

Footsteps sounded, and she turned toward the open doorway. A tall, dark-suited man entered the interview room. He flashed his badge. "Ms. Greco? I'm Special Agent Malone."

She fidgeted in her seat. He carried himself like a federal investigator, but he wasn't pseudotough. He seemed naturally intense, with dusty-brown hair threaded with an early-forties hint of gray, a chiseled nose, a square jaw and blue eyes. So dang blue, she stared straight into them.

This wasn't good. She wasn't prepared for the FBI agent to bewitch her. But he was.

She extended her hand. "You can call me Alicia." She didn't want to be Ms. Greco. She wanted to hear him say her name.

The special agent shook her hand with a firm grip, his voice purposely professional. "Alicia."

She got the expected thrill. He made her feel safe and sexy at once. Of course he did. She'd always had a secret little fantasy about G-men, inspired by B-movie magic. Her DVD collection brimmed with gangsters, gun molls and government operatives.

He moved forward and occupied the other side of the table. The Fijian inspector had sat there, too. But he hadn't possessed Agent Malone's do-a-girl-at-midnight dominance.

To keep herself from babbling, Alicia drank more water. This was the most nerve-racking day of her life.

The G-man got down to business. "It's my understanding that you recognized the victims."

"Yes."

"Will you tell me about that? The night in the disco?"

She'd already relayed her story to Inspector Inoke, but she assumed that Agent Malone wanted to make his own report. Then it hit her. He must be the profiler Zoë had told her about. The local papers had made mention of him, too.

"Are you the agent from the BAU?" she asked. She knew about the Behavioral Analysis Unit from movies and TV. "The profiler, right?"

"Technically, there's no such job classification as profiler. But yes, I conduct behavioral profiles of unknown offenders."

"Then that makes you a profiler."

Agent Malone's lips quirked a fraction at her zealous deduction, as if her persistence amused him. Alicia wanted to see his smile take root, but the humor in his expression vanished as swiftly as it had appeared. Suddenly his blue eyes seemed haunted.

From the darkness that surrounded his job? From delving into the macabre minds of the psychopaths he profiled? Or did something in his personal life torment him? She glanced at his left hand to see if he wore a gold band. He didn't. Neither did she. Not since her divorce.

The agent watched her watching him, and silence skittered between them. Her nerves ratcheted up again.

This interview wasn't going well. He probably couldn't wait to get rid of her. Of course she hadn't even answered his first question.

"The disco," she said.

"Yes," he parroted. "The disco. What time did you arrive?"

"About ten. It was already crowded when I got there. I don't normally go to bars by myself, but I'm an evaluator with the Secret Traveler, and I'm assigned to the Siga Resort. It's been remodeled since its last rating, with lots of new amenities. The disco is part of the remodel. The Ocean Terrace restaurant is new, too. It has the most spectacular view…." She caught herself going off track. "Sorry." She put her near-empty water cup on the corner of the table and tried to be a credible witness. "The DJ played a lot of old Madonna. But it's a retro club."

"Is that what was playing when you noticed the victims? When you first saw them dancing?"

"Yes. 'Holiday.' It's a song from her first album. Are you familiar with it?"

He shook his head. Apparently he wasn't a Madonna fan.

She sang the first few lyrics for him, then stopped, realizing this wasn't a karaoke session. But even so, the words to the song wouldn't go away. "Holiday" was spinning like a broken record in her head.

"What was your impression of the victims when you saw them dancing?" he asked.

"They made me feel…" She shifted in her chair and released the air from her lungs. The inspector hadn't steered her in this direction. His questions had been more cut and dried. Was the special agent putting himself in her place, trying to see the victims through her eyes? To process their behavior last night?

"What did they make you feel?" he implored.

"Sensual," she responded. His piercing blue gaze became riveted to hers. For an inane moment, she wondered if he wore tinted contact lenses, if he used them as a ploy to hypnotize witnesses. She continued her story. "They were so beautiful, so flirtatious, so enthralled with each other."

"How closely were you watching them?"

As closely as he was watching her now, she thought. "I barely took my eyes off them." She blinked, frowned, fought a fear-laced tremor. "They looked different this morning. I didn't recognize the girl right away. It took me a few seconds to realize it was her."

"I'm sorry you had to see them that way."

"Me, too." She couldn't imagine having his job, being tied to death, to brutality, to murder every day.

"Tell me more about the disco. How long were you there?"

"About an hour. I had one drink, a tequila sunrise."

"Did anyone ask you to dance?"

"No." Suddenly she became aware of her appearance. She was still wearing her jogging suit. Her long, wavy, dark hair was banded into a messy ponytail. Her face was devoid of makeup. "I looked better last night.

I had on this little black dress, nice heels, red lipstick."
Was that information relevant? Or was she getting off
track again? "But I wasn't putting out the vibe. I kept
to myself."

The special agent didn't comment on "the vibe," but
he glanced at her mouth as if he were imagining her lips
plumped and painted.

"Did you notice anyone else watching the victims?"

"A lot of people were watching them."

"As closely as you were?"

"I don't know."

"What about a white male, six foot or so, strongly
built...not a muscle man, but still a guy who can hold
his own? Mid- to late-thirties, moderately attractive...
Does anyone like that ring a bell?"

"I don't know," she said again. "There were probably
a lot of white, moderately attractive thirtysomething guys
there. That describes half of the tourists in Fiji. Is that
what the killer looks like?"

"Most likely."

Meaning what? That the killer's appearance was
speculation? Something Agent Malone had created as
part of his profile? Of course the police probably knew
some of the killer's physical traits based on forensic
evidence, and what they didn't know had come from
Agent Malone.

"Unfortunately, I don't have a security tape from the
disco to show you," he said. "Their surveillance equip-
ment has been on the fritz for weeks."

"Should I knock some points off of my rating for
that?" she asked, making a silly joke.

"Could you?" he responded, sounding serious.

He continued asking her questions, and she answered the best she could. She tried to focus on the disco instead of the crime scene, but her focus scattered, back and forth, like television channels switching in her mind.

Alicia reached for her water and swallowed the last few drops. "After I saw the bodies, I wondered why they'd risked messing around on the beach. But I think it was exhilaration, a high from getting naughty at the disco. When they walked outside, they probably felt wild, hot, sexually invincible."

The profiler didn't respond. But he glanced at her mouth again.

"Sometimes I have fantasies," she heard herself say. "To do something crazy with a stranger." His eyes met hers, and, as if falling into some sort of trance, she tumbled into the depth of his gaze. "I have this thing for G-men. If a woman can't trust a federal agent then who can she trust? A man with a government badge, handcuffs, a gun…"

Once again, he didn't respond. He didn't say a word. By now, he was sitting back in his chair, both eyebrows slightly raised.

Lord have mercy on her stupid soul. Suddenly Alicia realized what she'd done, what she'd said. Her breathing accelerated, her heart pounded like a fist inside her chest.

Too late, she thought. Too late to knock some sense into her. All she could do now was try to restore her dignity.

She clasped her hands on her lap, twisting her fingers together. "I didn't mean that like it sounded. When I'm nervous, I jabber. I say whatever pops into my mind."

He went professional, overly so. "You've been through a difficult ordeal. I can ask Inspector Inoke to recommend a trauma counselor."

"No, honestly, I'm fine. It's not as if I want you to handcuff me to the bedpost or anything." She was digging herself a deeper hole, saying even more ridiculous things. The temperature in the small room seemed to be rising, and the oscillating fan blowing in her direction wasn't helping to cool her off. "I just think you're handsome, that's all."

His expression went deliberately blank, no "thanks for the compliment," no obvious emotion.

"I'll ask Inoke to recommend someone," he said. "Just in case."

Great. He thought she was getting delusional over him. "My trauma wasn't that bad. I'll be all right, Agent Malone."

"Are you sure?"

"Yes." She wanted to crawl under the table, to hide her discomfort, but she lifted her chin instead, proving, or so she hoped, that she was allowed to find him attractive. That Alicia Greco was a normal, healthy, red-blooded American girl. "Are we done here? Can I go?"

He nodded and handed her his card, in case she remembered seeing anyone who'd been watching the victims at the disco.

Alicia took his card and stood up to leave. When she walked toward the door, she could feel the profiler's intense blue gaze following her.

Every self-conscious step of the way.

Griffin occupied a window-seat table at the Ocean Terrace restaurant, prepared to order a late meal and mull over the events of the day. But no matter where his mind traveled, it ran straight into Alicia Greco. He couldn't stop thinking about her.

He shifted his attention to the sea. She'd been right about the view. It was spectacular.

When he turned back, he saw her, not in his mind, but for real. A hostess was guiding her to a table just a hop, skip and jump from his.

She noticed him, too, and she stumbled on her next step. He smiled inwardly, a major feat for Griffin. He rarely smiled in any capacity. The chatty brunette had a good effect on him.

Good?

Who the hell was he trying to kid?

She stirred sexual impulses. He envisioned lifting her straight off her feet and carrying her across the hotel block to his room.

I have a thing for G-men. When she'd told him that, he'd done everything within his power to behave like the cool, collected special agent he was supposed be. He made his living studying the behavior of other people. He wasn't supposed to lose sight of his own.

But he was, damn it.

As she followed the hostess, he studied her tourist-girl appeal. Her gypsy hair fell long and loose, and she wore a floral-print dress, a breezy number with thin straps and a flowing hemline.

She took her seat, tried not to look at him and failed miserably. So did he. Between the two of them, they kept stealing glances. He nodded in greeting, hoping that acknowledging each other would help. It did, but only for a second.

He analyzed her body language as she picked up her menu and scanned the entrées. She wasn't actually reading the selections. She skimmed the words without seeing them.

Griffin hadn't ordered yet, but he'd decided on vegetable tempura and chicken maki. The Ocean Terrace served Japanese food.

Alicia glanced up and their gazes locked. Hell, he thought. This was going to be one whacked-out dinner. He reached for his iced tea, and she went back to fake-reading her menu.

A moment later, the waitress came by his table. She flashed a big white smile and wrote down his selections. He gave her credit for being bubbly on the heels of a double homicide. Then again, Griffin deducted that the resort staff had been instructed to keep the tropical ball rolling, to prove to their guests that a little death on the beach didn't have to destroy your own personal paradise.

Regardless, he suspected that the waitress knew that he was an agent on the case, so some of her show was specifically for him. He'd become recognizable around the hotel. As for Alicia, a news clip of her had already appeared on TV. A picture of her had appeared in a late-edition paper, too.

She glanced up at him again, and he wondered if he should invite her to dine with him, if eating together would take the pressure off.

Why not? he asked himself. It was just dinner. A casual meal. Some small talk. That made more sense than staring at each other from different tables.

He stood up, recalling what Alicia had said about wanting to do something crazy with a stranger.

There was nothing casual or small-talkish about her admission. But that didn't mean Griffin was asking her to dine with him so he could make her fantasy come true. He was capable of controlling his impulses.

He approached her and she reacted, all wide-eyed and pretty. He tried not to obsess over her mouth. Her lipstick was red, probably the same shade she'd worn to the disco. Or maybe she favored a variety of reds. Maybe this shade was darker or lighter or glossier than last night's choice. He had no way of knowing, short of asking her.

"Would you like to join me?" he asked instead.

She seemed surprised. "Why? So you can talk me into trauma counseling?"

"I won't go that route, I promise." Then what route was he taking? What were his intentions? He was doing a lousy job of admitting what he wanted from Alicia Greco.

"All right." She came to her feet. "But you have to buy me a glass of plum wine. I love plum wine with Japanese food."

She smiled, and he wondered if her hair smelled as enticing as it looked, if she used one of those seductively scented shampoos that foamed and frothed and sluiced down her skin.

Damn. Now *he* was on the verge of a fantasy. Wet, naked, sudsy images. "Dinner is on me, too."

"You, or the FBI?"

"Me." The Bureau didn't pay for agents to wine and dine witnesses. And he needed to be careful. Already he was hungering to hold her, to kiss her, to slide, hard and heavy, between her legs. No matter how erotic sleeping with a stranger sounded, taking Alicia to bed was a bad idea, even if she was the first woman to stir his desire since his heart had shattered.

Since he'd found his beloved wife—his friend, his lover, his lifelong partner—bound and gagged and cold to the touch.

Chapter 2

While Griffin tempered the gut-clenching memory, he and Alicia sat down together.

"I'm Griffin," he said.

She smiled. "Nice name. I like it."

"Thanks."

Being referred to as Agent Malone during a candlelit dinner would seem odd. Then again, this entire scenario seemed odd. He felt as if he were on a date and painfully out of practice.

The waitress reappeared, and he ordered the wine. Alicia needed a few more minutes to look over the menu before she decided on a meal. The server said "Okay" and darted off in her colorful outfit.

Within no time, the wine was delivered, and Alicia chose beef kushiyaki as an appetizer and tofu with mixed vegetables as an entrée.

Once they were alone, she sipped her wine and sparked a bit of conversation. "So, where do you live?"

Getting-to-know-each-other questions, he thought. Somewhere in the recesses of his cobwebbed brain, he remembered this ancient ritual. "Virginia Beach."

She gestured to the picture-perfect view. "So you're used to the sand and the surf."

"Not quite like this. But being near the shore feels like home. Of course, I travel a lot."

"You already know that I live in Chicago, and that I travel a lot, too."

He nodded. He knew facts about her from the witness report he'd filed. "Sounds like you have a glamorous career."

"I wish. This is the first time I've been sent to an exotic location. I'm part of the B team. The A team got sick, so the B team stepped in and saved the day. Zoë, Madeline and me." She sipped a little more wine. "They both called me this evening after the news got out. They wanted to be sure I was all right."

"I know all about Zoë Conrad and how she and Sean Guthrie figured out the serial killer aspect of the case." He'd spoken to Sean on the phone. "I can't say I'm familiar with Madeline."

"Madeline is a petite blonde. She's originally from Manhattan. She's always so put together. Sometimes I'm in awe of her. I don't have that kind of polish."

Griffin gave a moment's pause. Why was an uptown girl working as a B-team evaluator? To him, something about Madeline sounded off. But Griffin was always looking for lies, for inconsistencies, for the worst in people. It came with the territory of his job. "You've got plenty of polish."

"Really? Thank you." Alicia beamed. "But I don't see how. I'm from an average suburban town in southern Illinois. Anywhere, U.S.A."

"Me, too. Only it was southern Ohio."

"Look at us. The special agent and the blabby witness. We have something in common."

Griffin almost smiled. His dinner companion was sweet and funny. But she was a bit too candid. He dropped the urge to smile. He could tell that she was about to reveal overly personal information.

"I'm divorced," she said, right on cue. "My husband's name was James. Jimmy. We were married fresh out of high school. Then last year, Jimmy got bored with commitment and slept with another woman. I was devastated." Pain edged her voice. "I had no idea that I was living a lie. I thought we were happy. I loved being married." She drained her wineglass, her tone still chipped, still broken. "What a cruel joke that turned out to be."

For Griffin, too. But the cruelty wasn't in being married. It was in losing his wife—the ache, the pain, the guilt of failing her when she'd needed him. His woman. His Katie. Sometimes he missed her so much he could barely breathe. Now the only person who kept him going was their twelve-year-old daughter, the only bright spot left in his heart.

The waitress brought the appetizers, and the conversation was cut short. But not for long. As soon as their server departed, Alicia picked up where she'd left off.

"I decided to change my life after Jimmy did what he did," she said. "I filed for divorce, then packed up and moved to Chicago. I landed the Secret job, and the rest is history." She nibbled on her appetizer. "I'm not the old Alicia anymore. I'm a newer, freer, more independent version. The last thing I ever want to do is get married again."

Me, either, he thought, but he kept quiet. Unfortunately, his silence made Alicia aware of their one-sided conversation.

"I'm talking too much, aren't I?" She fidgeted with her napkin, resetting it on her lap. "I'm sorry. I must be nervous again."

He attempted to put her at ease. "It's okay. It's my nature to listen."

"And to process what you hear?" She cocked her head to one side, her gypsy hair rioting around her face. "Have you been analyzing me?"

"Not consciously."

"Then subconsciously?"

"Maybe a little." Or maybe a lot. He'd been absorbing every word, every gesture, every inflection.

"Then profile me. Tell me why I fell for Jimmy all those years ago."

He raised his eyebrows. Nervous or not, the girl had spunk. "Are you sure you want me to do that?"

"Are you sure you can?" she challenged.

He snapped his fingers. "Like that. Relationship 101."

"Okay. Shoot. Give it to me."

This wasn't complicated. Alicia had provided him with enough information to make a textbook evaluation. "Jimmy pursued you during high school. He was the aggressor. He wasn't a troublemaker, but he was bold and flirtatious. He had bad-boy qualities without actually being a bad boy." Griffin lifted a tempura vegetable from his appetizer plate and dipped it into the accompanying sauce. "How am I doing so far?"

With obvious fascination, she scooted closer to the table. Apparently he was right on the money.

"Tell me more."

He ate the vegetable and contemplated Jimmy's background. "Your ex-husband came from a broken home. His father, a responsible, hardworking, nine-to-five guy, raised him. His mother walked away when he was in elementary school, maybe even before that. She wasn't a nester like most women. She was a party girl."

Alicia all but gaped at him. Apparently he was still on target. He'd been making educated guesses. But he'd already gotten a feel for Alicia, for the kind of man she would have married fresh out of high school.

Their entrées were delivered, and they both picked up their silverware.

"Should I keep going?" he asked.

"Yes, please."

"Jimmy was attracted to you because you were everything his mother wasn't, everything his childhood had been lacking. You were the ultimate nester."

"And why was I drawn to him?"

"Because he fit your criteria. Jimmy had been taught to work hard, to pay his bills, to be responsible. He was what you considered safe, a partner you could trust, that you could rely on. But that didn't mean he was dull. You thought Jimmy was sexy." Griffin paused, met her gaze. "Safe and sexy is your MO, Alicia. Whether for a husband or a one-night stand with a stranger."

"I was wrong about him. He wasn't someone I could trust."

"That's why it hurt so damn much when he fooled around. He caught you unaware. As you said, you had no

idea you were living a lie. But if you'd looked closer at your
husband, you would have seen the signs of discontent-
ment."

"I'm impressed with your evaluation of Jimmy,"
she said. "But I don't know if I like what you worked
up on me. I don't sound as independent as I should." She
winced. "And my MO is a little embarrassing. You got
that from me blabbing about why I was attracted to
you."

He cracked a smile. "You're right. I did."

She exaggerated her expression. "Oh, my goodness.
The special agent is enjoying himself. Who knew he
could smile?"

He gave her a pointed look, but he was teasing, too.
"Are you accusing me of being a stick in the mud?"

"No. Just serious." She was no longer kidding. Her
tone was no longer light. "There's something in your
eyes. They're so blue. So compelling. But sometimes
they seem haunted."

"Haunted?" He refused to react too strongly.

She nodded. "You have ghosts in your eyes, Griffin."

What was he supposed to say? That it was Katie she
saw? His wife? A woman who'd been executed for forty-
three dollars in cash, two LCD TVs, one home theatre
system, miscellaneous jewelry and the wedding ring that
had been on her finger? "I study crime-scene photos. I
analyze evidence. I recreate murders in my mind. Who
wouldn't have ghosts?"

"I figured that was it. But I thought it might be something personal, too."

After Katie had been killed, the Bureau recommended
that Griffin undergo grief counseling through the FBI

Employee's Assistance Unit, but even after all of those sessions, he'd managed to keep his guilt to himself.

"You know all about Jimmy and me," she said. "And I don't know anything about you."

"What's to know? Except I carry a badge, a Glock and double-lock handcuffs." He took a swig of his tea. "Agent McSafety."

"Now you're poking fun at my fantasy again."

"Am I?" So much for controlling his impulses. He craved solace from her touch. But not gentle solace. He wanted to lose himself inside her, to thrust hard and deep, to forget that he was hurting.

He dragged a gust of air through his lungs, and they finished their meals. He offered to buy her dessert, but she declined. With nothing left to do, aside from going dancing or walking on the beach or making it seem like a real date, they agreed to call it a night.

Alicia put her napkin back on the table, and his zipper went tight, his pulse pounding beneath his fly. She'd left lipstick patterns on her napkin.

Griffin glanced at her mouth, where only a hint of color remained. He wanted those marks on his body. He wanted her to brand him.

He paid the bill, fighting the urge to snatch her napkin when she wasn't looking and tuck it in his pocket, which told him how close he was to losing his sexual sanity. "I'll walk you to your room."

"Thank you. I'm in the third block."

"Oh, yeah? So am I."

"Really? You're staying at the resort?"

"I checked in a few hours ago." Determined to exorcise the sexual demons, he concentrated on his job.

"I arrived in the Pacific two days ago, and I've been traveling between American Samoa, Vanuatu, Tonga and Fiji."

"So you're working directly with all four nations?"

"No, just Fiji. They requested BAU services, and we go where we're invited, whether on U.S. or foreign soil. But either way, the other nations are cooperating with the investigation, trying to help however they can." He wasn't the only BAU investigator on the case, but he was the only on-site consultant. The rest of his team was in the States, and he conversed with them through secure phone, fax and e-mail communication. "This is my home base for now."

She made a grand gesture. "You certainly can't beat the setting."

He agreed. "Fiji has its charm." As they strolled beneath foliage-draped walkways, they passed the entrance to a tropical garden, a gated swimming pool and softly lit hot tub.

In the distance, music from the disco pounded into the night, and Griffin turned his ear toward the sound. He'd already interviewed the DJ, the bartenders, the cocktail waitresses and the bouncer who'd been on duty last night. The bouncer had provided the most detailed statement. He'd noticed the victims getting naughty on the dance floor, but he didn't recall anyone watching them. Of course the offender would have behaved in a quiet manner, and the bouncer had been keeping his eye out for rowdy patrons.

The closer Griffin and Alicia got to their destination, the less audible the disco became. Finally, the music faded, drifting into what seemed like nothingness.

They approached a two-story building constructed from indigenous timber. It looked identical to the other hotel blocks. "What floor?"

She pointed to the second story.

"Me, too," he commented, escorting her to the stairwell. The Siga Resort didn't have elevators, but few hotels in Fiji did.

They continued, and when she told him her room number, his zipper went tight all over again.

"I'm right next door," he said.

"Oh, my." She looked up at him. "How strange is that?"

"Maybe it isn't strange. Maybe the hotel manager put me next to you purposely."

"Why would he do that?"

"To make it easier to give us preferential treatment."

She considered his response. "To deliver complementary fruit baskets? To put extra chocolates on our beds?"

"The guest who found the bodies and the agent profiling the killer? Wouldn't you be giving us freebies? Wouldn't you instruct your staff to treat us like VIPs?"

"I suppose I would. But the hotel giving me special attention isn't good for my job."

"It's not good for mine, either."

"I know, but I'm rating the resort. And I'm supposed to do it impartially."

"Then maybe you should tell the manager who you are. That you work for the Secret Traveler."

"That would make him treat me like even more of a VIP."

"You're visible either way. You've already been on the news, and your name is going to appear in the paper for a while. A sentence here, a sentence there. Until the press dies down, you can't do much to escape it."

"That doesn't make me feel very secure."

"It'll be okay." Without thinking, he reached out and tugged playfully on her hair. "You've got Agent McSafety next door."

That was all it took. One tug. One flirtatious gesture. Suddenly they were staring at each other. The air between them grew impossibly thick. He took his hand away, but the damage had already been done. Desire traveled through his veins, lightning fast and quicksilver hot.

"I'll bet you've done it before," she said.

"Done what?"

"Had sex with a stranger."

He figured she was nervous again or she wouldn't have brought up her fantasy. But he couldn't save her. He was nervous, too. He was back to being fixated on her mouth.

"You have, haven't you, Griffin?"

He fought the urge to move closer, to kiss her. "No."

"You haven't? Not even before you were FBI?"

His interest in her mouth intensified, taking a dangerous turn. Would she put her head on his lap and pleasure him in that way? Would she let him do it to her? "I was a state trooper before I was FBI."

"A peace officer who didn't get himself a quick piece now and then?" A shaky smile, an anxiety-ridden curve of those sexy lips. "Sorry, bad joke." Her gaze locked curiously on to his. "I thought most men have done the one-night thing."

He was half-hard and on the verge of getting harder. "I guess you thought wrong."

"I guess I did." She fanned her hands in front of her face. "Is it muggy out here or is it just me?"

"Our rooms are air-conditioned. Maybe we should go inside."

"Maybe we should. My clothes are sticking to my skin."

"Mine, too." This was the strangest, most oddly arousing conversation he'd ever had. They were talking about sex between strangers, but neither invited the other to partake in what was fast becoming a mutual fantasy.

She removed her keycard from her purse, and he took his out of his pocket, preparing to part ways.

"Sleep tight," he told her.

"You, too."

He waited for her to go first. She did, fumbling with the lock.

"Do you need some help?"

"No, I can…" She fumbled again, unable to turn the light from red to green. She tried a few more times. "There." She got it, pushing open the door.

They said goodbye once more, and she glanced back to look at him, quite longingly, before she went inside.

Griffin used the keycard to his lock. The light turned green immediately. He went into the empty room, removed his jacket and unholstered his gun.

Then he glanced over and realized that his room was connected to Alicia's from inside with double doors, one on his side and one on hers, designed for family or friends who wanted to share their accommodations.

Now she seemed even closer than before. All they had to do was unlock both doors to be together.

So what the hell was he waiting for? It wasn't as if he was going to compromise the case by sleeping with her.

No, but screwing around wasn't in his nature, either. He wanted Alicia to make the first move, for her to encourage him to sweep her into frenzied passion.

Griffin had been lovingly married for fifteen years, and heart-wrenchingly widowed for two. "Wham, bam, I'll do you fast and dirty, ma'am," wasn't part of his vocabulary. Yet that was how he wanted it to happen with Alicia.

He glanced down at his fly and cursed. By now he was raging hard.

Hungry for a woman he barely knew.

Alicia gazed at the door that connected her room to Griffin's. Some independent woman she was. This was her chance to fulfill her fantasy, to sleep with a stranger, a G-man, no less, and she'd let him slip through her fingers.

Maybe she could call him and invite him over for a nightcap. That would be a good excuse, wouldn't it? She had a minibar in her room. Of course he probably had one in his, too. If he was hankering for a drink, he could pour himself a quick, stiff belt.

Yes, but that wasn't the point. She was trying to find a clever way of getting him into her room and into her bed.

He wanted her, didn't he? It sure seemed as if he did, especially when he'd touched her hair, when electricity had zinged between them. Even those haunted eyes of his had turned hungry.

She could imagine him devouring her right up.

So do it, she told herself. Call his room. Or his cell phone. The number was on the card he'd given her this morning.

A cop turned FBI agent who'd never had a one-night stand. Alicia almost felt as if she were corrupting him.

But dang it, she needed this affair, her first fling, her first rite of passage. She needed to prove that she was wild and free.

She sat on the edge of an ornately carved chair and glanced around. The Siga Resort had been designed for tropical trysts. The bed was big enough for an orgy and the veranda showcased a moonlit sea. But best of all were the complimentary condoms in the bathroom.

Alicia dug Griffin's card out of the desk drawer where she'd stashed it and dialed his cell phone. One. Two. Three. She counted the rings, then his voice came on the line.

"Agent Malone."

Her breath rushed out. "Hi. It's me. The girl next door. I'm, um…" At a loss for words, she thought. Where was her chattiness when she needed it? "I was wondering if you wanted to come over and have a nightcap…or something."

He didn't hesitate. "The 'or something' sounds good."

"It does?" Warm chills slid down her spine. Apparently he knew exactly what she was up to.

"Unlock the inside door," he said.

"You, too."

"I will." His tone was deep, rough, perilously sexy. "Should I bring the cuffs?"

Oh, my God. What had she gotten herself into? "I don't—"

"I'm teasing you, Alicia."

"Oh, okay." Now she didn't know who was the corrupter and who was the corruptee. He was probably going to bend her every which way but loose. "I just need a second to get ready."

They ended the call, and she dashed to the bathroom to brush her teeth and fluff her hair. She removed her shoes, too, hoping to look more casual, more relaxed.

How about a quick spray of perfume? Or would that be too obvious? Would the fragrance lay heavy in the air? No, it would be fine, she thought, if she didn't overdo it. She used her favorite scent and waved her arms, trying to keep the floral aroma light and breezy.

She caught a glimpse of herself in the glass. She looked like a pelican preparing for flight. She dropped her arms and smoothed the front of her dress, tugging the neckline so it revealed a hint of cleavage.

Think Bond girl, she told herself. Sleek, sophisticated.

Something was missing. Lipstick, she decided. She needed to refresh the racy red color. She even pumped it up a bit, adding a silvery dot of gloss for shimmer and shine.

Alicia returned to the bedroom and heard the click of Griffin's inside door. The man had perfect timing. She unlocked and opened hers, too.

Boom!

There they were, face-to-face, with an illicit promise between them. Although he'd removed his jacket, his crisp white shirt, black trousers and leather loafers remained. His hair looked as if he'd carelessly run his hands through it, but the spiky brown strands didn't deter from his special-agent vibe. He still had it, all the way.

"Damn, you're beautiful," he said.

"Thank you." She stepped back so he could cross the

threshold and enter her room. "Do you want that drink, by any chance?" Something to slow the moment down, she thought. Her heart was racing so fast, so furiously.

"I just want you."

Nerve endings exploded. She pitched forward, and he grasped her hips and pulled her flush against him. He had a big, blasting erection. She felt it through his pants.

Still dizzy, still reeling from her own pounding heart, she flung her arms around his neck, preparing to be kissed.

And kissed she was.

Alicia's G-man nearly swallowed her whole. His tongue invaded her mouth, mimicking the driving motion of lovemaking. She returned his ardent fervor, and they got passionately sloppy, Frenching like teenagers in the back of a car.

But she didn't care. Nothing had ever felt so good, so forbidden, so wrongly right.

He backed her against the nearest wall, and they grinded through their clothes. The friction was almost more than she could bear.

He pulled down the front of her dress, just enough to expose more cleavage. As he cushioned his face against the fullness, she plowed her fingers through his hair.

"All I want to do is make you come," he said.

Oh, goodness. Oh, sweet heaven. She clawed his scalp, and he yanked her dress all the way off. Her strapless bra and lace-trimmed panties came next.

If she'd had the sense to be shy, this would have been the time to blush. He stepped back to study her, and she tried to envision what he saw.

A brown-eyed, wavy-haired brunette with her breasts held high and her stomach quavering.

"Open your legs, Alicia. Widen your stance for me."

She did his bidding. She let him dominate her. This was the most thrilling night of her life. She wondered if she would be begging to be handcuffed by the time he was done with her. Or maybe she would be begging to be held, to be warm and pliant in his arms. He was powerful, but he was gentle, too. He moved forward and kissed her again, only this time, he did it softly, romantically, as if another side of him had kicked in and taken over.

Who was he? she asked herself, as he triggered a myriad of emotions.

Who was Special Agent Malone?

Chapter 3

Alicia wasn't able to answer her own question. But it wasn't supposed to matter, was it? Griffin was her G-man fantasy, her sleep-with-a-stranger independence. Other than his job status, he was allowed to be a mystery.

But still…

Those warm, tender kisses, those hot, hungry hands. How could he be so reverent yet so passionate? So gentlemanly yet so wicked?

"Don't move," he told her.

"I won't." She stood right where she was, and he kissed his way down her body, leaving trails of wetness.

"So sweet…so soft…" he whispered against her flesh. He seemed to be breathing her in, absorbing her in visceral ways, starving for the texture, the scent, the erotic pleasure of being so close to a woman.

Thank her lucky stars that she was that woman. Her

skin tingled with every delicious touch. He toyed with her nipples, sucking one and then the other, rolling them between his teeth. Her head fell back and almost bumped the wall.

Alicia braced herself, putting her hands flat against the surface behind her. He whispered again, but she couldn't make out the words. All she knew, all she felt, was the flutter of his breath and the anticipation that went with it. He was moving lower.

Griffin dropped to his knees, and her heart skipped a thousand thundering beats. The willing-to-be-ravished witness and the famished agent.

He licked her belly and swirled around her navel, dipping into the indentation. He stopped to look up at her. His eyes glittered, feverish blue.

"Tell me what you want me to do to you, Alicia. Say it out loud."

"I want…" She tried to respond, but her voice was on the brink of shattering.

"Say it."

Suddenly she felt as if she were sacrificing herself to a stranger, giving him part of her fantasy-driven soul. "I want what you want."

"For me to make you sigh? And shiver? And scream?"

"Yes." Oh, yes.

He grasped her hips and pulled her against his mouth. She bucked on contact, her knees going wobbly. She reached out and clutched his shirt, fisting the fabric.

Alicia was naked, and the man on his knees remained fully clothed, doing explicit things with his tongue.

It was sexy. Oh, so sexy. But was this a safe way for her to feel? Trapped within his power? His voracity?

No, she thought. It was dangerous. *He* was dangerous.

Or was he? He gentled his hold and nuzzled between her thighs, making the act seem dreamy and idyllic. Alicia sighed, the sound drifting like a melody.

Sweet mercy, he confused her.

Achingly slow kisses, then…bam! He conquered her again, pushing her to the edge of peril. He licked the nub of her desire, over and over, shooting sparks deep within her core.

Taking her further, so much further, he planted his aggressive hands on her butt and nudged her forward, making her ride his mouth.

Alicia couldn't stop herself if she tried. She rocked her hips, and in her mind's eye, the room rattled and spun, the crash of the sea roaring beyond the walls of the resort.

All she could think was more…more…more.

Griffin gave her what she wanted, what she craved, and she took what he offered. Dazed, she whimpered, then moaned, then convulsed her pleasure, panting his name while he pushed her to orgasm.

As soon as the shuddering subsided, he scooped her up and carried her to bed. She landed on the mattress, and he climbed on top of her and kissed her squarely on the mouth, giving her a forbidden taste of herself.

He raised his head and shadows fell across his face. She wanted to follow the rigid contours, to trace his features, but he moved away from her to peel off his clothes.

Impatient, he tugged at the buttons on his shirt. She sat up to watch, fascinated by the roughness with which he stripped.

He bared his chest, exposing solid muscles and a sprinkling of hair. When he reached for his belt buckle and undid it, Alicia's heart pounded up a storm. Soon Griffin would be inside of her.

The rasp of his zipper made her shiver, but before he removed his pants, he extracted a condom from his pocket. The wrapper winked in the light.

"Is that from the medicine cabinet in your bathroom?" she asked.

He nodded. "You should give the hotel extra points for supplying protection."

"I plan to."

He tossed it to her, and she caught it like a shooting star. But she'd already made her wish, and it was about to come true.

Off came his pants, shoes and socks, leaving him in a pair of Calvin Klein boxer briefs. She smiled to herself. The special agent wore designer underwear.

He took them off, and she sucked in a couple of panting breaths. His fully erect penis sprang free. She liked what she saw. She liked every inch of him.

"Keep that close by until we need it," he said.

Her mind fogged. "What?"

"The condom."

"Oh…okay." She put the protection on top of the nightstand and told him, "I haven't done this since the divorce. I've been on a few casual dates, but I haven't been with anyone in a year."

He gave her one of his overly intense looks, and she wondered how long it had been for him, but he didn't offer information.

Instead, he came forward and slanted his mouth over

hers, kissing her the way he'd been kissing her all along, only now they were both naked.

Griffin released her, and air feathered in and out of her lungs. His flesh was warm and hard, his body in direct line with hers.

She wrapped her hand around his length, and he groaned his appreciation, muscles rippling down the center of his stomach. She stroked a little harder, and beads of fluid leaked onto her fingertips.

When she decided to lower her head, to take a salty taste, he nearly flew off the bed. One flick of her tongue, and he was toast.

"Your mouth," he said, as if she'd triggered a fantasy he was struggling to control. "Your lipstick."

"Do you want me to do to you what you did to me?"

"Yes. No." His butt flexed, his hips jerked and he yanked her up. "Where's the condom?"

She grabbed the packet and handed it to him, and within seconds he tore open the protection, sheathed himself and wedged between her legs.

Dang, she thought, chills smattering her body. Agent Malone was quite the multitasker.

Slam. Bam.

He thrust full hilt, and Alicia reached back and grappled for the headboard, preparing to white-knuckle the wood. Apparently Griffin couldn't handle any more foreplay. He needed sex.

Fast, forceful, coupling.

He did her so hard he rattled the bed frame. She arched her hips and took the exquisite pounding. No, she thought. She didn't just *take* it. She *thrived* on it.

He gunned her with blinding pleasure, all the way in,

then halfway out, then back in. They rolled over the bed and tumbled the covers, biting, kissing, going feral. She clawed his back, gouging him with excitement.

Somewhere in the midst of the mania, she climaxed. He'd maneuvered her body, angling her in such a way that he hit her G-spot.

G-man. G-spot.

She couldn't stop shuddering. As blood pulsed through her veins, as she splintered at the seams, another orgasm slammed into her. This time he used his fingers to make it happen, still pumping toward his own release.

She held tight, locking her legs around his waist. His gaze bored straight into hers, flashing like cobalt fire. He came in a burst of power, and the sound he made rumbled from his chest and echoed in Alicia's loins.

Afterward, he remained in position, still braced above her, his breathing labored, sweat glistening on his brow and making his hair stick to his forehead. Alicia was slick with perspiration, too.

She tried to think of something bright or witty or flirtatious to say, but her brain failed. Griffin didn't utter a word, either. There was nothing.

Nothing but awkward silence.

It seemed too late to congratulate each other on great sex. To say, "Hey, that was fun, let's do it again sometime."

The ghosts in Griffin's eyes had returned.

He frowned, but a second later he lowered his head to kiss her, softly, gently, as if he thought it was the right thing to do. That only made the moment more awkward. He hadn't severed their connection. Their bodies were still joined.

He finally spoke. "Do you want me to stay? Or go back to my room?"

She wasn't about to ask him to stay, and she suspected that he was too much of a gentleman to leave on his own, even if that was what he probably wanted to do. "You can go."

He withdrew, and she felt empty inside, not just physically but emotionally. But what did she expect from sex with a stranger? She should have known that there wouldn't be an afterglow.

He left the bed, but she didn't watch him dispose of the condom or get dressed. Alicia sat up and pulled the quilt to her chest. When she finally looked at Griffin, he was almost completely clothed. He'd put his underwear, pants, shoes and socks back on. As for his shirt, he'd left it unbuttoned, but was wearing it just the same.

He came forward to sit beside her. "Are you sure you're okay with me leaving?"

She clutched the covers a little tighter, keeping herself from touching him, from igniting false intimacy. In spite of his concern for her, he remained as uncomfortable as she was.

What had she been thinking, having her first fling with a haunted man who studied human behavior? She lifted her chin, trying to fool him, trying to look less vulnerable. "I'm a big girl, Griffin. I can handle being by myself."

He moved away from her, giving her the freedom she claimed to need. "Then I'll let you get some sleep."

"Thanks." She put on a brave smile. "I'll see you around, McSafety."

"You, too." His smile, even as slight as it was, didn't ring any truer than hers.

He left through the adjoining doors, closing and locking his door behind him. She got out of bed to do the same thing and noticed her clothes on the floor. She left them where they lay and climbed back under the covers.

A truly independent girl would've jumped in the shower and washed away the sex, but she didn't want to rinse Griffin's scent from her skin.

Alicia turned off the light, rolled over and hugged her pillow. She was going to have to work on the independent side of herself. But at least she'd lived out her fantasy and slept with a hot, hammering G-man.

She squeezed her eyes shut, and as darkness loomed around her, she was reminded of how and why she'd crossed paths with a special agent.

Because she'd found two bloodied bodies on the beach.

She opened her eyes and turned on the light, but the victims' familiar faces wouldn't go away. She saw them, shape-shifting into patterns on the ceiling and morphing into shadows on the walls. She glanced toward Griffin's room, wishing she'd swallowed her pride and asked him to stay.

Alicia slept fitfully, tossing and turning most of the night. At one point, she'd awakened with the covers wrapped around her like a body bag, a confinement that had left her gasping for air.

But at least morning had arrived. She climbed out of bed and grabbed her robe. As if daylight was any comfort. Sunrise creeped her out, too. The beach was never going to be the same.

She considered knocking on Griffin's door. Maybe he'd been right from the beginning. Maybe she needed trauma counseling. Or maybe she just needed to get naked with the FBI again.

G-man therapy?

She smiled at the thought. But a moment later, she frowned. One-night stands weren't supposed to carry over into the next day. Nor was she supposed to be thinking of Agent Malone as her personal protector. It wasn't his job to bank her fears.

She tightened her robe, walked onto the veranda and gazed at the sea, then at the long strip of pearly-white sand that followed the horizon.

The best course of action was to go jogging again, to prove that the beach wasn't a place to fear, to prove that she could get past this.

Alicia went inside and got dressed, slipping on an oversize T-shirt and a pair of shorts. She laced up her shoes and banded her hair into a ponytail.

She left her room and spotted a morning edition newspaper on a room service tray left outside of another guest's door. She wasn't interested in reading it. Already she could see that the front page featured an article about the murders. Had her name been mentioned? Probably. What had Griffin said? A sentence here, a sentence there? Luckily her picture hadn't been reprinted.

She took another glance at the headlines and noticed that the victims' names hadn't been released yet. She couldn't help but wonder who they were, where they lived, what kinds of jobs they had. Was this their first trip to the Pacific? Had they met in Fiji? Or were they already long-time lovers? Maybe even husband and wife?

Alicia got to the bottom of the stairs, inhaled a deep breath and headed for the beach. Although it was quiet, it wasn't as isolated as it had been yesterday morning. But it wasn't as early, either. A few other tourists were scattered along the shore, collecting shells or splashing in the water. Were they having honest-to-goodness fun? Or were they on a secret deathwatch, pretending that everything was normal?

She ignored them and took off running in the direction of the dreaded cabana.

But when she got there, the spot where it had been was vacant. Other cabanas remained, but that one was gone. Of course it was. The police had probably dismantled it for evidence. If not that, then the resort had removed it. They wouldn't have left a blood-splattered shelter on the beach.

Now what? Should she head back to the hotel and call herself cured of the fear that plagued her? Or should she continue jogging?

She glanced up at the cliffs. She wasn't adventurous enough to go for a solitary hike, but she could certainly go a little farther on her run, to keep moving along the shore.

So that was what she did, convincing herself that she was enjoying the strain of muscle and the sweat beading on her brow. That someday she would be fit enough to enter a marathon.

But her bravado was short-lived. The farther away she got from the hotel, the uneasier she became. Alicia sensed that someone was behind her, running to catch up.

A reporter looking for a scoop? For a more concise interview than she'd given on TV?

Or was it…

Who? The killer pretending to be another jogger? No, she thought. That was stupid. That made no sense. But she ran faster anyway.

So did the person behind her. Closer…closer…

"Alicia!" A man's voice rang in her ears, ricocheting in the wind.

The use of her name only gave her a bigger chill. Everyone in Fiji probably knew who she was, reporters and killers alike.

She heard his footsteps gaining on her. But she wasn't about to stop, so she kept pounding the sand, running in a mindless blur.

"Alicia!" he called out again. "It's Griffin!"

Oh, God. She tripped in the sand and cursed, an immediate sting of tears flooding her eyes.

Relief. Humiliation.

The special agent appeared at her side in an instant, reaching out to help her up.

"You scared me!" she snapped.

"Calm down, Alicia."

"You were chasing me."

"I was going in this direction and I saw you ahead of me. So I ran a little faster and called out your name. The last thing I was trying to do was scare you."

She finally took a minute to catch her breath, to encourage her heartbeat to stabilize, to wipe the embarrassing moisture from her eyes. "Maybe I overreacted. But I couldn't help it. I'm still spooked from yesterday."

He frowned, his hair blowing across his forehead. "Then what are you doing way out here?"

She glanced past him and noticed how far away from the resort they were. "I was trying to get over my fear."

"Well, you're doing a lousy job of it."

Shifting her gaze, she stared him down, scanning the length of him. He wore a mesh T-shirt, lightweight shorts and a pair of pricey running shoes. She should have known that he was a runner. Of course, he probably did strength training, as well. Agent Malone was in fine form.

He roamed his gaze over her, too, and as memories of being naked in his arms engulfed her mind, she blocked the sensual images. She didn't want to get obsessed with him, to crave him every time he got within breathing distance.

Too late, she thought, taking a step back.

"What exactly are you afraid of?" he asked. "Who did you think I was when I was running behind you?"

"A reporter." She responded quickly—too quickly?— and wished he wasn't looking at her with such acute awareness. "Or…I don't know, someone else…"

"The killer?"

"Yes, but then I realized that didn't make much sense. I mean, why would he chase me in broad daylight? Or why would he chase me at all?" She waited a beat. "He wouldn't be interested in me, right?"

"Truthfully? He's curious about you. By now, he's seen you on TV and in the paper. But he's curious about everyone associated with this case. And so are scores of other people," he added. "These types of investigations fascinate the masses."

She sat down in the sand and rubbed the goose bumps on her arms. "Gee, thanks. That makes me feel a lot better."

The special agent followed her to the ground, and

they both faced the ocean. "No one was chasing you, Alicia."

Except for the profiler, she thought. She turned to look at him. "Exactly how curious is the killer? About the case, I mean."

Griffin looked directly at her, too. "He's enjoying the media flurry, thriving on the attention he's getting. That's why he's killed twice in Fiji. Why he broke his pattern of keeping his crimes in separate island nations, the way he'd done before."

"He likes being a celebrity in Fiji?"

"An anonymous celebrity. He isn't trying to get caught."

"Do you think he remembers me being at the disco? Do you think he noticed me?"

"It's doubtful that a woman keeping to herself would have caught his attention." The agent's intense blue gaze pierced hers. "But you didn't notice him, either."

"Did anyone?"

"Not that we're aware of. But he's a chameleon. He knows how to blend in."

In an attempt to relax, she sifted sand through her fingers. As always, Griffin continued to watch her. But she was watching him, too. "Does the BAU ever make mistakes?"

"Of course we do. Profiling isn't an exact science. But we're right more often than we're wrong."

She didn't want to think about the times they were wrong, so she went with the premise that Griffin was right, that he was able to penetrate the killer's mind. "Why does he go after couples when they're having sex?"

"He's punishing them for flaunting their affairs, for

doing it where anyone could come along and catch them. Sex is evil to him. Dirty."

She turned silent, and so did Griffin. The physical intimacy they'd shared last night wasn't evil or dirty, but in their own way, they'd punished themselves for it. When the consume-each-other climax had ended, so had their comfort level.

Before the conversation stumbled to a complete stop, she said, "I've never seen anyone messing around in public."

"Because you're not looking for it. He's always ready, always waiting, always watching. And in this type of setting, he's going to find it."

This type of setting.

The tropical warmth, she thought, the grassy cliffs, the scent of flowers wafting through the sea air. "The South Pacific *is* intoxicating."

"Yes, it is." The sun shimmered in his hair. "It's affecting me, too. I thought about you last night."

Her pulse tripled. "You did?"

He nodded. "After I went to my room, I regretted not staying with you. I even woke up thinking about you, wondering if you would go for a run this morning, wondering if we would cross paths."

"So this wasn't a chance meeting?"

"I don't know. Maybe it was. Maybe it wasn't. All I know is that when I saw you, I wanted to touch you again. But I ended up scaring you instead."

"You're not scaring me now." Liar, she thought. She was afraid of how he made her feel, of how badly she wanted to touch him again, too.

Right here. Right now.

On the same beach where desperate lovers had died.

Chapter 4

"I'm dying to kiss you," Griffin said. He wanted to lean forward and cup Alicia's chin, to slant his mouth over hers, to take a forbidden taste.

She shivered, as if trapped between lust and fear. "Don't say 'dying.'"

"Sorry, bad word choice." But he couldn't think of anything else to describe how he felt. "It doesn't matter, because I can't let it happen." This wasn't the time and certainly not the place to unleash his urges. "Not here."

"We could go back to our rooms," she responded, making a surge of warmth shimmy to his groin. "We could be together there."

Any second now, he was going to get hard. "And do more than kiss?"

Her breath hitched. "A lot more."

Brrrring!

Griffin's cell phone rang, buzzing like an alarm clock in his shorts pocket, halting his near state of arousal. Alicia jumped back, reacting as if they'd just gotten caught with their clothes askew. She smoothed her baggy T-shirt, tugging on the hem and pulling the fabric in a flat line against her curvaceous body.

He retrieved the blaring device and checked the display. It was his daughter.

"I have to take this," he told Alicia, leaving their liaison waiting in the wings.

She nodded and let go of her T-shirt.

He walked away for privacy and answered the call.

"Hey, Pumpkin Pie," he said into the receiver, using the nickname he'd given his baby girl, Shauna, on the day she was born.

"Hi, Dad. I'm not bugging you, am I?"

He tried to keep from getting emotional. Since he'd arrived in the Pacific, he'd spoken to Shauna every day, sometimes two and three times a day. He understood how often she needed to hear his voice when he was away. He needed to hear hers, too. "Of course not. I'm glad you called."

"What are you doing?" she asked. "Are you at the police station in Fiji?"

"I'm out on a run, but I'll be going to the station later." Griffin stole a glance at Alicia. He'd bedded a beautiful witness last night, and this morning he'd had to refrain from kissing her on the beach, which, just yesterday, had been the location of a crime scene. This was some run.

"Grandma and Doris took me shopping," Shauna said.

He returned his attention to the phone. Doris was the

live-in housekeeper and trusted fifty-eight-year-old nanny he'd hired to care for Shauna after Katie had died, and the grandmother she referred to was Griffin's mom. His parents still lived in Ohio, but they always made the drive to stay with Shauna when he was out of town.

"What'd you buy?" he asked.

"Clothes. Some sparkly necklaces."

Griffin supplied Doris with credit cards to use for Shauna, and his folks were notorious for spoiling their granddaughter. But he didn't care what kind of girlish fluff Shauna bought, as long as it made her happy. Or as happy as a young girl could be who missed her mother. Sometimes when she cried about Katie, he thought his heart might break.

"After we got back, Doris dropped Jen and me off at the movies."

Jen was the best friend. Her dad worked as a U.S. Capitol police officer, and her mom was a Virginia PTA president. Griffin and Katie used to socialize with them. But these days, he kept to himself.

"What did you see?" he asked.

"Nothing you would have liked."

"A tween flick, huh?"

"Jeez, Dad. Can you make it sound any dumber?"

"A tweenager flick?"

She laughed, then went somber. Too serious for a girl her age, he thought. But her personality had changed since her mother had been murdered. So had Griffin's. They were different people from who they'd been before.

"Make sure they catch the bad guy in Fiji," she said.

"I will." His daughter was old enough to understand

the nature of his work. In spite of what was depicted in movies and on TV, profilers didn't apprehend criminals.

His job was to analyze offenders and suggest proactive techniques that might help the police catch the bad guys. But that was good enough for Shauna. She treated her daddy like a hero. But Griffin didn't feel the least bit heroic, not when he thought about Katie. He felt hollow and guilty. And lonely, he thought. So damn lonely for his wife.

"Have you met any hot girls, Dad?"

Damn. He glanced at Alicia. "Don't start in about my love life, Shauna."

"What love life? Everyone thinks you should start dating again. I think so, too."

"Oh, yeah?" he teased, trying to make light of a topic he wasn't prepared to discuss. "You're just trying to butter me up so I'll let you start dating or hooking up or whatever it is your generation calls it."

"There is a boy at school I like. Maybe…"

"No way."

She laughed. "That's what I figured. But really, it wouldn't hurt for you to go out once in a while. To meet someone new."

He didn't respond, so she dropped it, letting him off the hook. She said, "I better go now. Doris is making dinner, and Grandma and Grandpa are going to make ice cream for dessert."

"Enjoy your meal." On Shauna's side of the world, it was a day earlier and heading into evening. "And tell everyone I said hi."

"I will. Call you tomorrow, Dad."

"I love you, Pumpkin P."

"I love you, too."

They said goodbye, and he realized how long he'd left Alicia sitting by the shore.

He approached her, and she glanced up. She remained seated on the ground while he towered over her.

Should he tell her that he'd been talking to his daughter? Griffin frowned. If he told her about Shauna, then he would have to mention the child's mother, too. He would have to admit that he was a widower.

Alicia stood up and dusted sand from her bottom, and he slipped his phone back into his pocket.

"I get a lot of calls," he said, for lack of a better conversation.

"You're a busy FBI guy."

Damn it, he thought. He couldn't stand here and behave as if he were a childless bachelor with no responsibilities.

"That was my daughter," he said, preparing for what came next. "Shauna. She's twelve."

Clearly surprised, Alicia blinked. "I guess that means you're divorced." As she gauged his troubled expression, another thought seemed to spiral through her. She took a step back. "Oh, my God. You're not still married, are you? Please tell me that I didn't sleep with a—"

"I'm not cheating." He held her gaze, facing her with the truth, with words that nearly stuck in his throat. "My wife passed away two years ago."

"Oh…oh." Instant sympathy gentled her voice. "I'm sorry. I'm so sorry."

People were always sorry, he thought. Other than that, no one knew what to say. But he was sorry, too. Seeing Katie all dressed up in the casket had affected him almost as badly as finding her body. The funeral had given him no peace. For Griffin, there was no closure, only grief and guilt.

"I'd prefer not to talk about her," he said.

"I wasn't going to ask. I wasn't…" She chewed her bottom lip, sucking it between her teeth. "Am I the first woman you've been with since…?"

He nodded, forcing himself to tackle this discussion. "My daughter suggested that it might be time for me to start dating again, but she's just a kid. She doesn't know what's right for me."

"Is sleeping with me right for you?"

"It seems to be. I seem to need it."

She moved a little closer. "I seem to need it, too."

"Then do you want to pick up where we left off?" he asked. "And head back to our rooms?"

She smiled, obviously trying to keep things light, to bypass the emotion that loomed in the air. Behind her, the ocean foamed in crested waves. "Are you propositioning me, Agent Malone?"

He tried to sound playful, too. But he could have easily growled his hunger. "Yes, ma'am, I am."

"Well, then." She batted a long, dark curl away from her face. A few rebellious strands of hair had come loose from her ponytail. "My answer is yes."

His shampoo fantasy shot out of the dark and into the sun. "We're going to have to hit the shower. We're going to have to get wet and soapy."

She took the intended bait. "Is there any other way to get clean after a long, hard run?"

"Not that I know of."

"Then let's go."

With that, they ran, side-by-side, in the direction of

the hotel. Day-old strangers, he thought, anxious for a second helping of each other.

Arousal burned with every stride. He wanted to run faster, but he knew she wouldn't be able to keep up with him, so he went at her pace.

When they reached the stairs, he could have taken them two at a time. Alicia was winded, and he hadn't even broken a sweat.

"You okay?" he asked.

She nodded, and they each entered their own rooms, preparing to meet in the middle.

As soon as they unlocked the adjoining doors and came together, she kissed him with mighty force.

Oh, yeah, he thought, she was okay. She was just fine. They stripped each other where they stood, but they were too damn eager to care about their lack of finesse. His shirt got momentarily stuck while she pulled it over his head, and a few seconds later he battled with her sports bra. While she shoved her greedy hands down the waistband of his shorts, he went after her panties.

Another rough kiss, and he said, "Let's use your shower."

Her voice was breathy. "What's wrong with yours?"

He removed the ponytail holder from her hair, and the thick dark strands tangled around his fingers. "I'm curious about your shampoo."

"I didn't bring the brand I use at home. I'm using the little bottles the hotel provides."

He tugged her head back for yet another kiss. He wasn't letting his fantasy go. "Then my shower is fine. But I want to watch you wash your hair."

"Whatever you say. Whatever you want." Her nipples grazed his chest. "As long as you do me afterward."

Damn. He put his mouth to her ear and gave the lobe a quick nip. "Just lather and rinse, and I'll take care of the rest."

Drunk with desire, they stumbled to his bathroom. Griffin retrieved a condom from the medicine cabinet and put it on the side of the tub. After turning on the spigot, he adjusted the water temperature and climbed in the shower with his new lover.

They kissed under the rainlike spray. He couldn't seem to get enough of her tongue inside of his mouth. This was different than what he'd shared with Katie. With Alicia, he focused on the lust, not the relationship…the fantasy, not the reality. He'd been married for so long, he didn't know what uncommitted sex was like.

Even prior to Katie, he hadn't taken girls he barely knew to bed or into the shower or wherever. He dated them for a while first. He'd always been what women considered boyfriend/husband material.

But not anymore. At forty-one, he was done with commitment. Messing around felt good. Damn good. A willing divorcée at a tropical resort was just what the doctor ordered.

They soaped each other down, getting naughty while getting clean. Water bounced off of her and onto him. He handed her the shampoo and stepped back, moving completely out of the way.

She gave him a beautiful show, lathering her gypsy hair. The liquid foamed between her fingers, and his penis strained toward her.

Down, boy, he thought. Give her a chance to rinse.

She did, closing her eyes, the shower streaming over her hair and onto her skin. She had tan lines from sunbathing, making those areas of her body more noticeable.

The moment, the very instant she completed her rinse, Griffin grabbed her and pulled her tight against him. He kissed her, just once, before spinning her around.

With an excited gasp, she braced her hands against the tiled wall. Her wet hair hung down her back, nearly reaching her tailbone.

As he cupped her breasts from behind, steam gathered in the air, clouding the tub enclosure and frosting the glass. He breathed it in, thick and hot.

"Are you ready for me?" he asked, sliding one hand down to her belly, then along her cleft. By now, he was nestled against her bottom.

She didn't respond, but he didn't expect her to. He knew damn well she was ready. She was slick and wet.

"Stay there," he said. "Just like that." He moved away from her to tear open the condom and put it to good use.

Griffin returned and covered her like a rutting buck. She arched her body to give him better access, and he drove himself home.

Being inside her consumed him. He lifted her hair out of the way and licked her neck, tasting water-dampened skin. She pushed back against him, reacting to his deep-seated strokes. Increasing the tempo, he circled her waist and thrust harder.

"Come for me," he said, using his fingers to enhance her pleasure.

A moan escaped her lips. "You, too."

"I will." For her. Sweet, sultry Alicia. A woman he'd met yesterday. Was he losing his mind?

Yes, he thought. But he didn't care. Being naked with her soothed the ache in his ravaged soul—a quick fix, a hot, thundering balm.

Alicia made frenzied sounds, and Griffin's vision blurred, his loins vibrating with every thrust. The slap of flesh against flesh echoed in the mist, and he inhaled her into his pores.

She turned her head, and they fought the position they were in and tried to kiss, their mouths making jerky contact.

Bang…bang…bang…

His heart mimicked the driving rhythm of his hips. He went off like a rocket, and so did she. They climaxed at the same time, their bodies in sync…lovers, strangers erupting in passion.

Heaven on earth, Alicia thought. Griffin knew how to make her convulse. He withdrew, and she turned to face him, getting her postorgasm bearings.

He shut off the water, and in the breath-panting silence, she looked into his eyes, then did the unthinkable and searched for the haunting. She found it, locked deep inside him.

Agent Malone wasn't a complete mystery anymore. Now she knew something about him aside from his job. He had a twelve-year-old daughter and a deceased wife.

Had she lied earlier? Would she have asked him about his wife if he'd allowed her to question him? She honestly didn't know. There was part of her that was desperately curious about the woman he'd married—the woman he'd obviously loved. But another side of her was afraid of his pain. She couldn't bear to think of Griffin as a loyal husband, grieving for his past. That would only make her feel closer to him.

The wrong kind of close.

Upon stepping out of the tub, he handed her two towels. He said, "I want to keep doing this."

She used the first towel for her hair and the second for her body. "Sleeping with each other while we're in Fiji?"

He got rid of the condom and dried off, too. "Yes."

"So do I." At least she understood his hunger. He'd been celibate for two years after he'd lost his wife, and she'd refrained for a year after her divorce. Between the two of them, they couldn't help themselves. "Good thing our rooms are connected." Sharing their accommodations would make the intimacy more accessible, and in spite of her fears, she wanted him. "How long will you be in Fiji?"

"I'm not sure. It depends on how the case unfolds."

"I've got about two weeks left, then it's back to Chicago for me. But you probably already know how long I'll be here. I think I said it on TV during that jumbled interview I gave."

"Yes, you did." He turned toward the mirror, terry cloth tucked around his waist. "But you and I can get a lot done in two weeks."

She knew he meant a lot of bumping and grinding. She was tempted to invade his towel and bring him back to arousal. But she behaved herself.

He ran his hand along his jaw. "I need a shave."

"Do you want me to leave?"

"It's all right if you stay."

"Then I'll hang out for a few minutes." She stood back and observed him, dizzy with the newness that went with having an affair.

"What's on your agenda today?" he asked.

"I'm going to have breakfast in the diner, then head out for a golf lesson. The golf course is part of my rating, too. Everything is."

"Everything?" From the mirror, his gaze snared hers. "Does that include me?"

Alicia's emotions skittered, and she struggled to feel like the single, free-spirited girl she was supposed to be. He looked so husbandly, standing there, getting ready for work. "You're a five-star agent."

"I better be."

"Believe me, you are." She watched him buzz his beard stubble with an electric razor. Afterward he tapped on some cologne, and she inhaled the woodsy scent. "Would you like to have breakfast with me?"

"Thanks, but I'll grab something near the station. How about if we do dinner? Maybe order something from room service?"

"That sounds good." Perfect for a cozy rendezvous. "I'll see you later."

"All right."

Before she left, she caught a glimpse of the ghosts in his eyes, and the darkness that surrounded him gave her an instant chill. She adjusted her towel and walked away.

But she changed her mind about leaving so easily. Turning around, she went back to him, pressed against his long muscular body and kissed him deeply.

In response, he snaked his arms around her, pulling her even closer. "Damn, woman. You're making me want you again."

"You're supposed to want me again. That's what

affairs are supposed to be about." After one last kiss, she slipped away and returned to her room, satisfied that she would be on his mind for the rest of the day.

As Griffin sat in a cluttered office at the police station with crime-scene photos scattered across the desk, his thoughts kept wandering.

To Alicia.

She knew exactly what to do to drive him mad. He wondered how they could be so sexually compatible, so physically right for each other. The laws of attraction, he supposed. Pheromones. Chemistry.

He glanced at the photos. According to the investigation, the couple who'd been slashed had had undeniable chemistry, too.

A shadow hovered in the open doorway, and Griffin glanced up, almost expecting to see their corpses floating toward him.

He caught sight of Inspector Inoke instead. The officer sported a *sulu,* a gabardine skirt that was part of his traditional uniform. In Fiji, it was men's formalwear. But *sulus* could be casual wear, too. For men and women.

"How'd it go?" Griffin asked. Inoke had met with the victims' families that morning.

The inspector cleared his throat. He stood about five feet ten with deep brown skin, thinning dark hair, a full face and a neatly trimmed moustache. "It's always the worst part of our jobs."

It was worse for the families. Griffin knew firsthand what being in both positions was like. From a law enforcement point of view, murder was a subject to study, to analyze, to solve. But from a family's perspective, it

was an impregnable wall of pain, a few short, dark steps
from hell. Having a loved one die a violent death went
beyond the realm of reality. "Did you release the victims'
names?"

"They'll be on the news in the morning."

"That's fine. But I'd like to discuss something else
with you."

"Go ahead."

"We haven't had any new witnesses come forward,
but it's been next to impossible to locate everyone who
was at the disco that night. It gets a lot of tourist trade
from other hotels, too. It's a popular nightspot."

Inoke scowled. "Sometimes I think our UNSUB isn't
an unknown subject, he's an unknown phantom."

"He's real. We just need to find someone who noticed
him."

"Maybe he wasn't at the disco. Maybe he came across
the victims at the beach."

"No. He was there. He watched them dance." Griffin
couldn't say how he knew the UNSUB had been at the
disco, other than instinct, other than a gut feeling he'd
learned to trust. "But I think he left the club before they
did, waited somewhere in the dark for them to come out,
then followed them to see where they would go from
there. To the hotel. Or the beach."

"They should have picked the hotel."

Should've. Could've. Would've. How many times had
he wished that he could go back in time? "People don't
get those kinds of second chances."

"Things like this make me want to go home and hug
my kids." Inoke lifted a photograph, a close-up of the
female victim's neck. Had the cut been any deeper, she

would have been decapitated. "She left behind a son. A three-year-old. I saw him today, clinging to his grand-mother."

The Fijian inspector had never dealt with murders of this magnitude. Serial killers weren't part of his society. This case was hitting him hard. But Griffin understood about hugging your children. He understood it well. You couldn't tell your kids that monsters didn't exist because you knew the truth.

"There were a lot of tears," Inoke said. "Breakdowns over identifying the bodies."

The air in Griffin's lungs went tight. For now, he couldn't bear to think about the families. Soon he would be meeting with them, too, looking into their eyes and feeling their pain.

He changed the course of the conversation, getting back to the investigation. "What do you think of foren-sic hypnosis?"

The inspector dropped the photograph back onto the desk. "I've never had call to use it. Why? Is that what you wanted to discuss with me?"

"I think it might help." He'd come up with the idea after he and Alicia had parted ways this morning. "I've got a witness in mind who might make a good subject. Under hypnosis, she might remember significant details from the disco."

"Who?" Inoke made a talking motion with his hand. "The chatty American who found the bodies?"

"Yes."

"She's sweet, that one."

Griffin wasn't sure if the inspector meant sweet as in nice or sweet as in sexy. Knowing Inoke, he meant both.

Either way, Griffin wasn't about to admit that he was sleeping with her. Eventually the inspector would figure it out. He was too observant not to.

Did getting found out even matter? Two weeks from now Alicia would be back in Chicago, and Griffin would return to being a companionless widower.

He refocused on the case. "If your department is willing to try hypnosis, I can discuss it with the witness, and if she's agreeable, I can arrange to bring a forensic hypnotist in from the States."

The other man didn't hesitate. "We're willing. Do you think your girl will go for it?"

His girl. Maybe Inoke knew already. Maybe Griffin had it written all over his face. Lord only knew, she occupied his thoughts. But she wasn't alone. Katie and his daughter were there, too, along with the killer he was profiling and the people whose lives had been taken. What could he say?

Except that his mind was a crowded place.

Chapter 5

"You want someone to hypnotize me?" Alicia gazed at Griffin, her nerves jumping like little beans in her stomach. She had expected him to return from the station in a romantic mood, to order dinner and make use of one of the two beds at their disposable, but he hadn't even loosened his tie. "What if I do something stupid while I'm under?"

"There's no such thing as 'being under.' Not in the way you mean it." He led her to the empty dining table in her room, and they sat across from each other. "Hypnosis is an altered state of consciousness that seems like a sleeplike trance, but the subject is fully alert, more so than normal. Hypnosis requires you to focus. You'd be in control of what you're doing and saying."

"The hypnotist can't make me bark like a dog?"

A smile tilted Griffin's lips. "He can suggest it, and

if you're easily led, you might decide to do it. But it would still be your choice."

"Woof," she said, and made him laugh.

She laughed, too, thinking how gorgeous the special agent looked when he enjoyed a bit of humor. His haunted eyes actually twinkled.

But not for long. He turned serious again.

"Some people aren't susceptible to hypnosis," he said. "There's no guarantee that it will work. But when it is effective, the subject is more likely to recall details that eluded him or her in a conscious state, and that's what we'd be looking for from you."

"If I agree to do this, would you be there with me?"

"It's just the hypnotist and the subject during the actual session. But I'd be nearby in another room."

"Would the session be audiotaped?"

"Yes. We'd have a forensic artist on hand for afterward, too." He shifted in his chair. "If you want to try it, we'll make it as easy and comfortable as possible for you. And if you prefer to decline, that's perfectly okay, too."

"No pressure," she said.

"No pressure," he repeated. "This isn't about us, Alicia. It's about the case. So whatever you do, don't base your decision on me."

"I won't."

"Just take some time to think about it, and get back to me when you decide."

"Okay. Do you still want to order dinner tonight?"

He nodded. "Do you?"

"Absolutely."

"Then let's see what they have."

They scanned the room service menu and chose the same meal: fish boiled in coconut cream sauce with indigenous vegetables on the side.

While they waited for dinner, Griffin remained in his work attire. "I'm not going to go overboard trying to hide our affair," he told Alicia. "But I'd just as soon not advertise it, either."

"No mussed hair or robes or unmade beds in front of the hotel staff?" she surmised.

"Or kissing in public," he added.

"What about sex on the beach?" she asked, cracking one of her typically bad jokes and making him shake his head. Still, they both ended up laughing—the second time that night. She was on a roll.

After the food arrived and the server departed, Griffin shed his tie and undid the first few buttons on his shirt. Alicia got more comfortable, too.

"I think Inspector Inoke already knows about us," he said.

"Wow. That was fast."

"Cop intuition. But truthfully, I don't think he gives a damn who I'm boning as long as I remain focused on the case."

She couldn't help herself. She bit back a smile and put him in the hot seat. "Boning?"

"Sorry." The gentleman in him emerged and he winced accordingly. "I didn't mean it like that."

"It's totally okay." She didn't mind being the subject of his improper language. It made her feel decadent, a woman who inspired hard, fast sex and the words that went with it. Wasn't that better than being Jimmy's emotionally distraught ex-wife?

"It's not okay. We might be playing around, Alicia. But you're still a nice girl."

Dang. Now he was making her feel as if she were someone he was meant to care about. He never failed to confuse her. But she suspected that she confused him, too. They were both new at this.

She clutched her fork, warning herself to retain her independence. The husbandly side of him made her long for her old home-and-hearth ideals, the marriage-and-babies tale she'd once believed in.

Alicia scorned herself for her foolishness. What was she going to do? Marry Griffin and help him raise his daughter? Oh, sure, she thought. And while she was at it, she could get pregnant, too. That would serve Jimmy right for having a low sperm count, for not giving her the children she'd wanted so badly.

They ate in silence, until she said, "When they cleaned my room today, they left a voucher for a complimentary massage at the health spa."

"They left one in my room, too."

"You were right about the hotel giving us freebies."

He watched her with a complex expression, as if he were still caught up in her being a nice girl. "We don't have to use the vouchers."

"No, but I wish the hotel would treat me as they would any other guest." She smiled a little, trying to seem unaffected by his stare. "A free massage does sound good, though."

"Yes, it does."

He said it as if he meant it, and she realized that he *did* mean it. But he wasn't talking about getting rubbed down by a hotel masseuse. His eye contact turned sexual, and desire tripped through her veins. She forgot all about marriage and babies and being a nice girl.

Griffin wanted her for the same erotic reason she wanted him. And now, all they needed was a bottle of island-scented lotion or oil or whatever they could find to boost their pleasure.

For the rest of the night.

Griffin awakened to the warmth of a naked woman next to him. God, how he'd missed this feeling. Fast asleep, Alicia was nuzzled in the crook of his arm, her tousled hair tickling his chin.

They'd had one crazy night, greasing each other down and making love like maniacs. Before the lubrication fest, she'd used her luscious mouth on him, and he'd watched her. Bound by her teasing, her petting, her sucking, he'd experienced a rush of hot, slick sensations. He couldn't wait for it to happen again. She fulfilled every fantasy he could fathom.

But there was more to Alicia than sex. He'd seen the vulnerable side of her, the little bird who'd lost her nest. Like now, he thought, as she lay curled against him. She seemed to need him, to feel safe in his arms while she slept.

Her ex had been a self-serving jerk to hurt her so carelessly. Griffin would never have cheated on his wife. No, but that didn't give him the right to play the almighty until-death-do-us-part husband.

He closed his eyes, and the past hit him with blunt-tipped pain.

"Don't go," Katie had said to him that weekend. Whenever Shauna was away at summer camp, Katie wanted to spend quality time with Griffin, to sleep until noon, to make love on a whim, to take nighttime walks, to snuggle in front of the TV with a pint of Ben and Jerry's.

"I have to," he'd responded, even though he'd elected to go out of town. "I'll make it up to you when I get back."

She'd smiled and said okay, as if she'd wanted to believe him. He'd made the same kind of promises in the past, but most of the time he got too engrossed in his work to keep his word. This time, he'd gone a step further and offered to take her on a romantic vacation as soon as his schedule was free.

Two days later, he'd returned and found her body.

How could he have done that to the woman he loved? How could he have left her home alone to be bound, gagged and shot?

Alicia moaned in her sleep, and Griffin flinched and opened his eyes. Then, feeling overwhelmingly protective, he tightened his hold on her, as if he were holding on to Katie. He knew what he was doing was wrong, but he couldn't seem to let go.

She woke up and lifted her gaze to his, and they stared at each other in soul-jarring silence.

Alicia wasn't his wife. She wasn't Katie. But still, he held on. He even lowered his mouth and kissed her, quite reverently, as if she belonged to him.

"Sometimes you scare me," she said afterward.

"You scare easily," he responded, and released her.

"Maybe I do." She sat up and gathered a portion of the sheet around her. "Or maybe you're just the most intense man I've ever met."

"Yeah, I know. I've got ghosts and all that. But I'm not expecting you to chase them away."

"No, of course not. This is just an affair." She studied him as if she were thinking of moving back into his embrace.

He waited, watching her, too. Little by little, she surrendered, inching closer, and it was all he could do not to curse her cautiousness, even though he had no right to get possessive. A few more scoots and she caved in, letting him loop her into another powerful hug.

"Just an affair," she reiterated.

Griffin had already been through this in his own mind. Eventually their liaison would fade into a distant haze, but for now it blazed in spinning colors.

He kissed her again, only rougher, more ravenous this time. Even so, the tongue-to-tongue contact didn't merge into sex. She didn't roll over on top of him, and he didn't snag a condom from the nightstand where the protection was now being kept. They separated and stared at each other in that soul-jarring way again.

The colors spun a little faster, and he shook his head to make them go away.

A moment later, they both roused from bed, and she made a pot of coffee. She offered him a cup of the percolating brew, and he refused.

"I don't drink coffee."

"Oh. Okay."

After that the quiet between them was deafening, but when she picked up the remote control to turn on the TV and create noise, he stopped her with a simple command.

"Don't," he said.

She frowned. "Why not?"

"Because the victims' names are being released this morning, and I don't want to watch it right now." He would see it later. Griffin viewed all of the news clippings over and over on tape. He studied them intently, analyzing how the killer would react to each report.

"I'd like to know who they are." Alicia sipped her coffee as if she needed the warmth, wrapping both hands around the cup. "If I know their names, maybe they'll become something other than the bodies I found." She searched his gaze. "Will you tell me about them?"

Griffin nodded. There was no way he could deny her request. He understood how traumatic this was for her, not just the murders, but getting involved with him, too. Her G-man fantasy was more complicated than she'd counted on.

She settled in to listen, sitting on the edge of the bed. He opened the blinds and exposed the veranda, making their surroundings brighter, hoping it would help.

"Her name was Veronica Phillips, and his was Paxton Knight," Griffin said. "They were fashion models. They came to Fiji for a photo shoot, and when their job was over and the rest of the crew went back to the States, they stayed for another week."

"So they could be together?"

"Yes."

"Did they meet on the shoot?"

"Yes," he said again. "They weren't quite strangers, but they didn't know each other very well, either. It was still new."

"Veronica and Paxton." She mulled over their names. "I should have known they were models. They were so beautiful. How old were they?"

"She was twenty-two, and he was twenty-four. She has a three-year-old son with an old high school boyfriend."

Alicia made the same sad face Inoke had made when he'd told Griffin about the boy. "I'm so sorry for what happened to them." She put her coffee on the nightstand, steam swirling from the cup. "I want to do it. I want to be hypnotized, to help identify the killer if I can."

He sat down next to her, then reached out to skim her cheek. "I'll arrange it as quickly as I can."

"I'll be ready." She leaned into his touch. "I'm never going to forget Veronica and Paxton. If I live to be a hundred, they're going to stay with me."

"You're going to remember them even more vividly after the hypnosis."

"I know. But it's okay. I'm doing this for them."

She put her head on his shoulder, and he slipped his arms around her, keeping her close.

As if he were holding Katie once again.

For Alicia, the next two days went by in an emotional blur, and now she rode shotgun in Griffin's rental car, which he was handling just fine. No way would she attempt to drive on the left side of the road.

She gazed out the window, steeped in her surroundings. Fiji consisted of three hundred and twenty-two islands, but only one hundred and six of them were inhabited.

Viti Levu, the island they were on, was the biggest and most populated. The highway they traveled passed a series of towns and cities with busy marketplaces, cinemas, shops, clubs, cafés, monuments and museums. But once Griffin got off the main road, the villages got smaller and less commercial.

They arrived at their destination, and he stopped in

front of a wood-and-straw *bure* located on a remote resort.

Traditionally Fijians had two types of houses, a *vale,* which was a family house, and *bure,* a house where men of the clan met. But in the tourist trade, the term *bure* was used for various types of detached hotel/resort structures, ranging from simple to extravagant.

"It's charming," she said.

"We thought you'd be more comfortable here than our hotel."

She knew he meant on a primal level. This was the place where she would be hypnotized. She noticed another vehicle parked amid the palm trees. Apparently the rest of their party was already there.

They exited the car, and as they walked to the front door of the *bure,* Griffin put his hand on the swell of her back. The gesture seemed natural, as if he'd done it hundreds of times before. But he hadn't. This was the first time he'd given her a lingering touch outside of the rooms they shared.

She glanced at his profile, warning herself, as always, not to get too attached. Their affair was deeper than she'd bargained for, but it was uncomfortably hollow, too. He'd yet to speak of his wife, and he protected his daughter. Shauna had called quite a few times over the past few days, and he always excused himself to take the calls, keeping the conversations private.

He took his hand away, and she prayed that she wasn't getting in over her head, that when she went home to Chicago, she wouldn't long to be back in his arms.

They entered the *bure,* and Griffin introduced her to Bob Roizen, a retired FBI agent trained in forensic hypnosis. With his silvery gray hair and thick white brows, he reminded her of the wizard in "The Wizard of Oz." He put her at ease immediately. Inspector Inoke and a sketch artist named Dan were on-site, too. He was the youngest of the group, probably around Alicia's age.

Bob led her to a small room in the back of the cozy dwelling that was furnished with a rattan sofa and several padded chairs. Instead of instructing her to recline on the sofa, he offered her one of the chairs.

She took a seat, and he assured her that he wouldn't be swinging a pendulum and chanting, "You are getting sleepy. Very sleepy." He chuckled and told her, "That only happens in the movies."

He explained that although her muscle activity would decrease and her breathing and heart rate would slow, her mind and senses would become more alert.

The session began with Alicia concentrating on the pattern of Bob's voice. He was no longer speaking in an animated way. The sound had become monotone, yet deeply soothing. He led her through what seemed like a quiet tunnel, where she was alone with his voice. Her feet seemed to be floating just above the ground, even though she knew that she was still seated firmly in her chair.

He kept talking, and soon she was walking into the disco, feeling as if she were in the midst of a lucid dream. The sights and sounds of the bi-level, retro-inspired club came vividly alive. Lights flashed in moonbeam colors, and the smell of body heat, perfume and alcohol wafted to her nostrils.

Madonna's voice vibrated from the sound system,

charging the crowd with eighties pop. "The DJ is playing 'Lucky Star'."

"Tell me about the other club goers," Bob—the wizard—said.

"They're mostly tourists, but there are a few hopped-up locals." In her mind's eye, she glanced around for a free table. "It's crowded. I'll have to stay at the bar."

"Can you see the dance floor from where you are?"

"Yes. But I can only see the dancers on the edges of it. I can't see who's in the middle." She told Bob to wait because the bartender, a big friendly Fijian, was coming by to take her order. "I'm getting a tequila sunrise with extra grenadine. I like them sweet."

"Tell me when the DJ plays 'Holiday.'"

Alicia knew that song was important because it had been playing when she'd first noticed Veronica and Paxton. But she hadn't known their names then. Of course she knew them now.

Her drink arrived, and she removed the orange-cherry garnish and placed it on a napkin. The glass was cool in her hand. "It's not playing yet."

"Then fast-forward to it," Bob said.

Holiday…celebrate… Just like that, the lyrics burst out of the speakers. "It's on."

"Are you watching the dance floor?"

"Yes. It's not as cramped now. I can see the people who were in the middle. Uh-oh…" Anxiety twirled in her belly. "There they are. Veronica and Paxton." She wanted to reach out and save them from their fate, but she couldn't.

"Stay calm, Alicia. Relax and tell me about them."

She listened to his suggestion, the anxiety diminishing. "They're so beautiful. They're like mirror images of each other. Their hair is almost the same shade of blond, and they're tall and sleek and tan. They even move alike." She swayed on her bar stool. "I feel like a voyeur."

"Why?"

"Because they're rubbing against each other, rocking their hips. Paxton has his hands on Veronica's butt, and he keeps pulling her closer."

The couple spun and turned, and Alicia leaned forward. "A button is straining on Veronica's blouse. I can see a flash of her bra." She wondered if Paxton's zipper was straining, too. His jeans were deliciously snug. "They're making me thirsty." She lifted the tequila sunrise and wet her mouth, mostly with ice. "Her clothes keep getting skewed. Every time he shifts his hands, her skirt raises a little. It's already a miniskirt, and it's getting shorter." Another ice cube taste. "I keep hoping they'll kiss."

"Do they?"

"No." The song ended and another began. "Borderline." More vintage Madonna. "Veronica just lifted her hair off of her nape, and now she's letting it slide through her fingers and down her back. Paxton looks as if he wants to eat her alive."

"Is anyone else watching them besides you?"

"A lot of people are. It's as if they're putting on a show for us." She glanced around the club. "A trendy Asian couple in the corner is checking them out. They have their heads together and they're whispering. But now they turned away to eat their appetizers."

"Who else?"

"The bartender has been glancing at them in between

pouring drinks, and two men on the other side of the bar are watching, too."

"What do they look like?"

"They're young, early twenties, with longish hair. They look like artists or musicians. One of them has a pierced nose, and the other has a goatee."

"Who else do you see?"

She described everyone within range.

"Are you going to get up and walk around?" Bob asked. "Or use the restroom?"

"No. I'm staying at the bar, sipping my drink." Which meant that she didn't have a view of the entire club. But she couldn't change what had happened that night.

"What about the second level? Can you see the patrons up there?"

"From what I can tell, it's mostly college students. They're making a lot of ruckus. They seem pretty drunk. The bouncer is keeping his eye on them." She turned to watch Veronica and Paxton again. She couldn't help it. She was drawn to their erotic energy.

The DJ announced that he was wrapping up the Madonna set with "Like a Virgin," and Paxton and his partner got even naughtier. The once-controversial lyrics seemed to set the tone, heightening the sexuality.

She glanced toward the door. "A man just walked in by himself." Oh, God. Her heart went erratic. "It might be him. The killer."

Once again, Bob told her to relax, and she stabilized. "Why do you think it's him, Alicia?"

"He fits the profile. He's white, probably in his mid-thirties, tall, athletically built and moderately attractive. He's wearing black slacks and black polo-type shirt."

"That's fine. Now describe him in detail."

"He has a high forehead, deep-set eyes, hooded eyebrows and a straight-bridged nose. His lips are thin, and he has a slight point to his chin." She paused, still staying calm. "His hair is short, like Agent Malone's, only a lot darker. It's not spiky, but it could be if he wanted to style it that way. Agent Malone's hair gets spiky when he runs his hands through it."

"What's he doing now?"

She knew Bob meant the stranger, not Griffin. "He's just standing there, sort of pressed against the wall. He noticed Veronica and Paxton right away. He appears to be watching her more closely than he's watching him. Veronica is lip-syncing the final chorus of 'Like a Virgin' and sliding her hands along her body. She's teasing Paxton."

"And the other man?"

"A middle-aged couple just walked in front of him, and they're blocking my view."

That was it. When the couple disappeared, so did the possible killer. He'd moved farther into the disco and out of Alicia's sight.

She shifted to look at Veronica and Paxton, who were hip to hip once more. "Van Halen's version of 'Pretty Woman' just came on. I think the DJ is playing it for Veronica. Or maybe it's for all of the women in the club. A group of college girls are coming downstairs to dance with each other."

She finished the watered-down remnants of her drink. "Veronica and Paxton are on the other side of the dance floor now. I can't see them anymore."

Bob asked her to tell him how the rest of the evening

unfolded, and she went through the paces of leaving the club and going back to her hotel room.

He reminded her to keep the man who'd been pressed against the wall fresh in her memory, so she could describe him to the forensic artist.

From there, it ended. The wizard talked her out of the hypnotic state as easily as he'd talked her into it, and she emerged with the Sex on the Beach Killer on her mind.

Chapter 6

Alicia spent three hours with Dan, the forensic artist, while he interviewed her and worked on the composite. She looked through a copy of the FBI's facial identification catalog, where face shapes, eye types, nose types, mouth types and other features were categorized. With the aid of this tool, she was better able to convey physical details about the man in the disco.

The final draft of the composite gave her a chill. She nodded her approval. "That's him. That's the man I saw."

Later, she and Griffin headed back to their hotel. Once again, she sat beside him in the car.

"Do you think he's the killer?" she asked.

"There's no way to be sure. But it's a place to start." He glanced her way. "You did good, Alicia."

"Thanks." She truly appreciated Griffin's praise,

especially after everything she'd been through. "What happens now? What are you going to do with the composite?"

"Use it to further our investigation." He turned back to the road. "A public memorial for the victims is being arranged, and it's our hope that the offender will make an appearance. We discussed this with the families and got their approval. The service will be covered by the press, but law enforcement will also be taping it and watching everyone in attendance. If the man in the composite shows up, we'll bring him in for questioning. We'll keep our eye out for anyone who could be the offender."

She considered their tactics. "Why would the killer attend a public memorial?"

"For the thrill. As soon as he hears about the event, he's going to fantasize about walking amongst the mourners as if he's a secret star going down the red carpet, but whether he follows through remains to be seen."

"I'd like to attend the memorial," she said. "If the man in the composite shows up, I'll recognize him right away."

"It'll be an emotional situation for you, Alicia. It'll be held on the beach where the murders were committed. A temporary structure is going to be erected for the service."

"In place of the original cabana?" She tempered her memories from that day, pushing the gruesome images to the back of her mind. "I can handle it. Besides, I'd like to pay my respects to Veronica and Paxton."

Griffin nodded his approval, and she could tell that he cared about the victims, too. Not just Veronica and

Paxton, but all of the couples the Sex on the Beach psycho had slashed.

"I don't know how you do this all the time," she said.

"It's my job. It's who I am. But that doesn't mean I couldn't use a break."

"Me, too."

"Then we're prime for what I have in mind." He kept both hands on the steering wheel, but he looked as if he wanted to touch her. "Do you want to go away on an overnight trip? Just the two of us?" He paused. "To a private island?"

She smiled at the romantic fantasy he'd created. "Of course I would. But I'd like to eat chocolate every day and not gain an ounce, too."

"I'm serious, Alicia."

"You are?"

He nodded. "An old friend of mine owns an international security company, and he provides secure homes all over the world, places his high-profile clients can go to escape. I called him this morning and asked if he had a property in the South Pacific I could use, and he offered me a private island retreat."

"Then let's do it." She could barely contain her excitement. Being alone with Griffin sounded heavenly. No hotel employees, no tourists, no reporters, no stress. "I can take a few days off."

"So can I. The police shouldn't need me until the memorial gets closer, but if they do, I'll be available by phone. I won't be out of touch."

Of course not, she thought. He wouldn't leave his work completely behind. If the cops called, he would be back in a flash.

"I figured this was a good way for us to spend some time together." He slanted her a sensual glance. "We're going to have lots of sex. We're going to do every wild thing we can think of."

His expression, his voice, his words jolted though her. She envisioned climbing onto his lap here and now, regardless of being in a moving car.

"I wouldn't have it any other way," Alicia said, and he slanted her another desirous glance.

In the erotic silence, she turned up the air-conditioning and adjusted the vents to maximize a cooler temperature. Even with a serial killer in their midst, with death all around them, they couldn't control the heart-hammering heat of each other.

The following morning, while Griffin was at the station wrapping up a few things before he and Alicia left for the private island, she got the urge to connect with her friends. Utilizing her time alone, she made a three-way call to Zoë and Madeline, her coworkers and best gal pals, so they could chat from their different island locations.

Zoë was relaxing with Sean for a bit, and Madeline was on her second resort assignment. Due to their relative experience, Alicia had been given just one resort to rate, and Madeline had taken on three. Or was it four? Madeline was ambitious that way.

"You're *what?*" Zoë asked at the height of the conversation.

"Sleeping with the profiler," Alicia responded.

"Talk about getting wrapped up in the case." This from Madeline. A second later, she asked, "So, give us the scoop, how is he?"

Ah, Alicia thought. Girl talk. How she loved it. "He's gentle and wicked and everything in between. I can't get enough of him."

"Sounds like Breeze and me," Zoë said.

Alicia's pulse spiked. Breeze was Sean Guthrie's nickname, and the man with whom Zoë had fallen completely in love. "No...no. It's nothing like you and Breeze."

"How can you be sure?"

"You're making a life with Breeze. This is just an affair."

The other woman responded, "We started off that way, too. But after our emotions got tangled up, I knew what we felt for each other went deeper. I fought it at first, but now I can't imagine a day without him."

Alicia gripped the phone a little tighter, and her jerky breathing puffed into the receiver.

Madeline piped up, "You're scaring her, Zoë."

"She was already scared before she called," came the experienced reply.

"I was not," Alicia jumped in and lied.

Zoë refused to buy her baloney. "You were, too."

Madeline spoke again, addressing Zoë once more. "Just because the profiler is poking her doesn't mean she's falling for him."

Alicia broke into a light laugh and so did Zoë. Thank God for Madeline and her city-girl wisdom. Alicia pictured the chic blonde, coiffed and polished, with every eyelash in place. But as glamorous as Madeline was, sometimes Alicia worried that her friend was lonely, that she took her aloofness too far. Then there was Zoë, a woman who'd been searching for adventure, but was now ready to settle down and become Breeze's bride.

"I should go." Alicia wanted to get off the line before Zoë, the happily betrothed, persisted and worked her over again.

The trio said goodbye, and she promised to call them again soon. After they hung up, she tried to clear her mind. But all she could see was a shimmering white dress and a shiny gold ring.

But that wasn't what Alicia wanted anymore. Right? Right. Been there, done that. Marriage was something out of her past.

She packed a bag for the getaway trip, and when Griffin returned and entered their adjoining rooms, her heart tripped into pitter-patter mode.

"Hey," he said, approaching her with a kiss.

He tasted like mocha latte. Yummy, she thought. She dived in for more, captured his tongue, then stepped back and said, "I thought you didn't drink coffee."

"I don't. It's hard candy." He reached into his pocket and handed her a paper-wrapped drop, twisted at both ends.

She opened it and popped it into her mouth. He watched her suck on the treat, and she got warm all over.

He removed his tie. He always wore professional attire when he was working. The consummate G-man.

"I need to change," he said.

Alicia nodded. She was already ready, having donned shorts, a lace-trimmed tank top and sandals.

Griffin stripped off his suit and put on casual clothes, too. Together, they looked like tourists, like a husband and wife on holiday. Alicia's stomach flopped and fluttered. She had to stop thinking like that.

Once they were outside, they both slipped on their sunglasses, and their excursion began.

They took a chartered Cessna float plane piloted by a man named Tom Laruso, a big, dark, wildly handsome American who obviously lived and worked in the Pacific. She wondered if he thought she and Griffin were husband and wife. If he did, she doubted that he cared who they were or why they were headed to a private island. He didn't strike up small talk. He stayed completely out of their business. In fact, he seemed a bit antisocial. Nonetheless, he appeared to be an excellent pilot.

After they touched down on the edge of a golden-sanded shore and exited the aircraft, Tom made a remarkable takeoff.

"He used to be a bodyguard," Griffin said.

She watched the float plane glide across the sea and go airborne. "Really? I didn't get the impression that you knew each other."

"We don't. My security friend arranged this flight. He's the pilot they use."

So Tom had brought other people to this island. The high-profile types Griffin had mentioned before. "He seems surly."

"Maybe he has ghosts, too."

Maybe nothing, she thought. Apparently Griffin had been informed about the pilot's background. He knew for certain that Tom had ghosts. "Did the security company tell him that you're an agent?"

"No. But he was told that I'd be armed. That's pretty much all he needed to know."

"Does he only fly security missions or can anyone hire him?"

"He's available for anyone. Why?"

"I'm going to recommend him to Madeline, so he can fly her to her next assignment. Or maybe even give her a tour of the islands or something. He's strong and tough, and I think he'd be good for Madeline."

Griffin watched the Cessna. "You're trying to set them up?"

Was she? Would perfectly coiffed Madeline appreciate Tom's rugged appeal? "I'd just feel better if she had a safe guy around." In case Madeline needed someone to lean on, in case she wasn't as independent as she led other people to believe.

In case the serial killed moved on to Madeline's resorts.

As the plane vanished, she fought to clear her mind and turned toward Griffin, trying to focus on the next phase of their trip. "So what happens now?"

"We wait for the caretaker of the house to pick us up." He glanced at his watch. "He should be here soon."

Within no time, a Polynesian teddy bear of a man arrived in an off-road vehicle. He introduced himself as Matareka and told them that his name meant "The one with a smiling face," which suited him perfectly. His big, white grin was infectious. He commented that he was married and that his wife's name was Ulani, which meant "Cheerful and lighthearted." Alicia suspected they were a happy couple.

He drove her and Griffin away from the shore and into a torrid jungle, where a winding dirt road had been roughly carved.

Then Alicia saw the private villa, surrounded by an iron gate.

They entered the property and Matareka gave them a tour. The house was exquisite, with its contemporary architecture and artistic decor, and the landscape was just as impressive. Set amid glittering greenery and scores of hibiscus was a lagoon-style swimming pool, a grotto spa and a man-made waterfall.

Matareka showed them that the fridge was stocked. He also handed Griffin the keys to a four-wheel-drive vehicle that was in the garage in case they wanted to return to the beach on their own.

"Just let me know if you need anything else," the Polynesian man said. He and his wife were the caretakers of the house, but they didn't stay on-site when guests were present. They would be at a cottage farther down the road.

"Thanks," Griffin responded. "We'll be fine."

Matareka smiled and bid them farewell, leaving Alicia and her FBI lover alone.

Griffin and Alicia put their luggage in the master suite, but they didn't test out the bed. Griffin had a different setting in mind.

"Let's go swimming," he said.

"Okay." She unzipped her overnight bag and rummaged around for her bathing suit. "This place is amazing. I wish we could stay longer."

"We'll just have to make the most of the time we do have." He was going to suggest skinny-dipping, but he thought it might be more fun to work their way up to that.

She found her suit and headed for the adjoining bathroom. "I'll be back in a flash."

"I'll be waiting." While she was gone, he changed into swim trunks and tucked a couple of condoms in the Velcro pocket.

Then, without warning, a stab of guilt boomeranged him, punching his heart into a tailspin. He'd promised Katie a romantic vacation, but here he was on a tropical island with another woman.

The bathroom door opened and out came Alicia in a pink crocheted bikini with her hair tumbling over her shoulders and down her back. Another boomerang. Only this time, the guilt was wrapped in a tight ball of lust.

"That's some swimwear." When he swallowed, or gulped, or whatever the hell it was he'd just done, he could feel his Adam's apple working along his throat.

"The color is called bubble gum." She smiled, putting a unique spin on his lust. "But it didn't come with a wax-paper comic."

Griffin moved forward, close enough to inhale the soft scent of her skin, to toy with the string ties on her bikini top. "Who cares about the comic? It's the gum I always wanted."

When he grazed her shoulder with his teeth, she asked, "Are you going to chew my bathing suit off me?"

Was he? "I think maybe I am." He nibbled on the fabric around her breasts, and her nipples poked against the lining that held the crocheted netting in place.

With his hands and his mouth, he loosened the string ties a little more, then scooped her up and carried her out to the pool, intent on tossing her in the water so her top would come all the way off.

She squealed, kicking and screaming. Her flirtatious protests made him feel like a teenager, crazy and ready for fun.

So why not take the plunge, too?

He ran toward the sparkling oasis and jumped in

with Alicia in his arms, and they hit the water in a flurry of foreplay.

Splash!

They went down together, separated, then reemerged for air. His plan of attack worked. She lost her bathing suit top. The skimpy pink garment floated away. With water dripping in his eyes, he grinned at her. She laughed and splashed him.

Needing more, they swam closer and kissed. She looped her arms around his neck, her breasts crushed to his chest. He cupped her rear and pulled her tighter.

Before they drowned in their own hunger, they got to the far edge of the pool near a corner seat where a waterfall burst in illuminating colors.

Climbing out of the water, they went wild on the decking. Alicia slid her hand down the front of Griffin's trunks and made him as hard as the rock formations around the grotto. He looked into her eyes and let her stroke him into a fever. But not without copping a hot, wet feel, too. He invaded her bikini bottoms and used his fingers deep inside her.

Twin moans escaped their lips. Together, they stripped, and Griffin kissed his way down Alicia's body and buried his face in the soft, moist juncture between her legs.

She pitched forward, and the taste of her sent sweet shimmers through his blood. He paused to run his tongue along her thighs, creating deeper sensations.

She writhed under his touch, and he made furious love to her with his mouth. Barely gripping the edge of his own sanity, he pushed her toward a convulsive release. She lifted her hips and bucked like a cowgirl, thrashing and trembling.

Griffin drank her in. All of her. But she didn't give him time to savor the triumphant feeling.

Before he knew what hit him, she managed to get between his legs, and the urgent pull of her mouth nearly sent him into sexual shock.

He tangled his hands in her wet hair, and while he watched what she was doing to him, he listened to the sensual rush of the waterfall spilling into the pool.

His erection pulsed, thumping like a heartbeat.

He grappled for the swim trunks he'd discarded, praying the prized condoms were still in the pocket.

As he fished around for the protection, she teased him. If he came too soon, it would be her fault. He was already leaking heavily at the tip.

Caught between glorious pain and primal pleasure, Griffin made her stop. He handed her a condom. "Put it on me." There was no way he could do it himself. He needed a spiraling second to breathe.

She managed the task without the slightest trouble. "Now what?" she asked, being coy.

He got control of his libido. "Now, we get wet again." In one swift move, he hauled her into the water with him. He was forty-one years old and had never made love in a pool. He figured it was about time.

They used the corner step. He sat down and glided her onto his lap. The penetration was thick and liquid carnality. He lifted her up and down, and her breasts skimmed his skin, her nipples tightening into hard little nubs.

A mind-buzzing concoction of tropical flowers and chemical-treated water permeated the air.

He couldn't imagine a more thrilling encounter. He filled her completely, her body welcoming his.

In…out…deep…deeper…

The longer it continued, the more he needed. Until, finally, Griffin closed his eyes.

And let a shuddering orgasm consume him.

Alicia opened her eyes and realized it was morning. She'd slept soundly beside Griffin. She peeked at him through her still-heavy eyelids, but she could only see the back of him. He wasn't facing her.

She leaned forward and kissed his bare shoulder, and he moaned huskily.

"I'm going to make breakfast," she said, keeping her tone soft and low. "I'll call you when it's ready."

"Okay. Thanks." His voice was raspy. "I like my eggs over hard. No runny yokes."

She smiled and let him doze, understanding why he was still tired. They'd made marathon love yesterday. She'd lost count of how many times he'd pursued her after their swimming pool liaison. Griffin had been ravenous, always wanting more.

She hoped he had the same appetite for breakfast, especially since they'd only snacked at dinnertime last night. She enjoying cooking, and she missed fixing meals for someone other than herself.

Uh-oh. Was that a wifely thought?

Determined to kick the marriage paranoia, she put on her robe and headed to the kitchen. So she wanted to cook for her lover? So what? He wasn't going to be her lover forever.

She brewed a small pot of coffee for herself and got cracking on the food, deciding to make eggs, bacon, fried potatoes with onions and bell peppers and waffles topped with fresh strawberries and whipping cream. When Matareka had told them the fridge was stocked, he'd meant it.

She suspected that Matareka's wife was the one who made sure groceries were available for guests, ordering supplies and keeping the kitchen in order.

Alicia envisioned her as a traditional woman, maybe because Matareka seemed like a traditional man. The marriage-minded type.

She shook her head. As if *she* were the authority on married men. The loyal little helpmate with the cheating spouse.

Alicia hadn't suspected a thing. When the woman Jimmy had been fooling around with called the house and said, "I'm sleeping with your husband, and I want him for my own," Alicia didn't believe what she was hearing.

In her naiveté, she'd automatically assumed the aggressive female had dialed the wrong number—until the other woman identified Jimmy by name.

But that was over and done.

Holding fast to her divorced independence, she finished breakfast and returned to the master suite to awaken Griffin, but he was already out of bed and zipping into a pair of khaki shorts.

He looked mussed and ruggedly handsome. Beard stubble shadowed his jaw and his hair was spiked from sleep. As he dragged a T-shirt over his head, she put on clothes, too, removing her robe in favor of a sundress.

He tamed his hair with a quick thrust of his hand. "The food smells good."

"It's going to taste good, too."

"Not as good as you taste."

"Griffin." He couldn't possibly be hankering for sex again.

"Wanna bet?" he asked and laughed.

She gaped at him. "Did you just read my mind?"

He gave her an I'm-a-profiler look, and she rolled her eyes and laughed, too. Then she went quiet. Alicia was fascinated by his ability to second-guess her, but sometimes it unnerved her. She wondered if it had bothered his wife.

Perish the wife thoughts, she warned herself.

But as they sat down to eat, and he complimented her on the hearty breakfast, she kept thinking about the woman he'd married.

He studied her from across the table, and she tried to lighten her thoughts so he wouldn't figure out what was on her mind. Then she decided to just go ahead and ask him about his family. But chicken that she was, she started with his daughter.

"Do you think Shauna will call you today?"

He alternated between bites of eggs and forkfuls of potatoes. "If she doesn't, I'll call her."

"What do you talk about so often?"

"Nothing in particular."

She lifted a slice of bacon. This conversation was off to a lousy start. But she should've known that he would give her generic responses, probably because he sensed the wife questions were coming later, and he was getting up his guard.

Still, she pressed on. "Do you have a picture of your daughter I could see?"

He paused, then waited another beat and nodded. "On my laptop."

Well, then. That was something. Although he'd been hesitant, he'd agreed to show her a photograph. But maybe the proud father in him couldn't resist. Luckily he'd brought his laptop along on this romantic side trip of theirs. But he probably always kept his computer with him.

Alicia figured that was enough questions for now. She would ask him about his wife after she saw Shauna's picture. That would be a good lead-in to the girl's mother.

Wouldn't it?

While they finished eating, they chatted about inconsequential things. Afterward, he helped her clear the table. They did the dishes together, too. She rinsed everything, and he loaded the dishwasher.

The domestic intimacy made her emotional, especially after they completed the task and Griffin came up behind her at the sink, moved her hair to one side and kissed the back of her neck. In spite of his admission earlier, it wasn't a sexual advance. He'd gone husbandly on her. But that was part of Griffin's nature, something that was deeply ingrained in him. She doubted that he could change it, no matter how hard he tried.

So, did that mean she couldn't change her wifely nature, either?

She turned to face him and their eyes met. Neither said anything, which only made the moment more intense. She wanted to put her head on his shoulder, to hold him, to never let him go.

As fear reared its anxious head, she revisited the conversation she'd had with Zoë and Madeline.

Was it possible for her to follow in Zoë's footsteps? To fall madly, desperately, crazily in love with Griffin the way Zoë had taken the tumble for Breeze?

Yes, she thought with a jolt of panic. It was possible. But how she would survive it went beyond comprehension.

"May I see the picture of your daughter now?" she asked, needing to know more about him.

He nodded, went into the bedroom and returned with his laptop.

While Alicia stood back, he placed the portable device on the kitchen table and booted up. She waited a moment and moved forward.

"This is my baby girl," he said, as a photograph appeared on the screen.

His baby girl. Alicia studied the twelve-year-old, with her long, straight, dark hair, deep brown eyes, tanned skin and sweet smile. "She's beautiful, Griffin." She continued to gaze at the image of her lover's child. "She has an ethnic flair. I always admired those types of features."

"Her mother was half Native American. Shauna is a quarter blood with the Choctaw Nation of Oklahoma."

Alicia's pulse tripped. She'd wanted to ask Griffin about his wife, and he'd offered a bit of information. "Her mother must have been beautiful, too."

"She was." He commented quickly, almost painfully, then switched the topic back to his daughter. "Shauna and I build sand castles together. We're pretty darn good at it."

"Really? That sounds fun." She had no idea how to segue back to his wife, so she didn't even try. "I've never made sand castles."

"Do you want to put on our bathing suits and head over to the beach? I can show you how it's done."

"I'd love to." She reached up to skim his jaw. But she didn't know if she was comforting him for the loss of his wife or comforting herself for being on the perilous verge of falling in love.

Chapter 7

When the moment got too tender, Griffin stepped back, deliberately creating an emotional distance. Anxious to get going, he instructed Alicia to help him gather supplies to take to the beach. While he sorted through gardening tools and buckets in the garage, she rummaged through the kitchen for plastic containers in various shapes and sizes.

He examined their haul. "This ought to do it."

"Gosh, I hope so." She laughed a little. "I had no idea we would need so much stuff."

"You want to build a nice castle, don't you?"

"Yes, of course."

He loaded the SUV and said, "Sometimes Shauna makes princes and princesses out of sand. People who live in the castles we build."

"She must be a dreamy girl." Alicia's wistful expression told him that he'd hit a childhood chord. That she used to fantasize about fairy tales, too. That she'd been obsessed with storybook love.

"Yes, she is. But a lot of young girls are."

"Did you always build sand castles with her?"

Griffin got behind the wheel as Alicia settled in beside him. He knew what she meant. She was asking if his wife had been involved or if it had become a father-daughter activity after Katie had died.

"No, not always," he responded, giving her the answer she was looking for without having to mention Katie.

Alicia went quiet. Before the end of the day, before they left the island, she would probably summon the courage to ask him direct questions about his wife. But he would avoid that when the time came. For now, he pushed it to the back of his troubled mind.

They arrived at the secluded beach and chose a spot a short distance from the shore, kneeling to spread out their building supplies. A warm breeze blew and the ocean rippled in blue waves.

"We're going to start with a foundation, a big mound of wet sand the size we want our structure to be. From there, we'll sculpt and create shapes." He looked in her eyes and saw her fascination, not just for the future castle, but for him, too.

Was she getting attached to him? Of course she was. He was getting possessive of her, too. Regardless, he leaned forward and kissed her. He would miss the silky warmth of her body next to his. He would miss her nervous chatter and cozy sweetness, too.

She returned his affection, and he absorbed the tender ache between them, running his hands along her spine.

When they separated, he fought to let go. Hell, he thought. Why did he keep doing this? Why did he keep holding her as if she belonged to him?

Maybe he needed to end the affair. Right now. This very instant. But he did just the opposite and kissed her again. Only this time, he did it as if the island was destined to explode and this was his last kiss on earth.

Griffin took her mouth with desperate force, dragging her flush against him. He didn't mean to be so rough, but he couldn't seem to stop the frustration that burst inside him.

He pulled away. "Ask me," he snapped.

Alicia braced her hands on her knees, fighting for balance. His abrupt retreat had left her teetering. "Ask you what? What's going on? What's wrong?"

"Ask me about my wife. You want to know about her, don't you?"

Her voice rattled. "Yes, but—"

"All right, here it is. She was murdered, and I found her body. I knew she was dead the moment I saw her, but I tried to revive her anyway."

"Oh, God." Her skin paled. "I'm so—"

"Sorry? Sometimes I hate that goddamn word."

She just stared at him, and he feared she might cry.

What the hell was he doing? This wasn't Alicia's fault, and now he was *sorry* that he'd snapped at her. He caught what was left of his breath, of his brutal stupidity. "Please, forgive me. I have no right to take this out on you."

The kindness in her glowed like a halo, and he felt like even more of a bastard.

"There's nothing to forgive you for, Griffin."

Oh, yes, there was. He needed absolution for leaving his wife alone that weekend, but he wasn't about to admit it aloud.

"Her name was Katherine," he said, keeping his voice calm. "But she went by Katie. She was killed during a home invasion robbery. It was a random act of violence. The offenders didn't know her or me. They weren't aware that an agent lived there. They were a couple of tweakers, meth addicts getting antsy for their next score." He inhaled a gust of sea air and continued. "I was out of town on a case, and Shauna was away at camp. Katie answered the door and two men forced their way inside. They knocked her unconscious, ransacked the house, then took everything they thought was of value, including the wedding ring she was wearing." Another breath. More air. "When she started regaining consciousness, they bound and gagged her and put her in a walk-in closet. Then one of them panicked about leaving a witness and shot her. Just like that. He killed my wife." One more pause. "He pleaded guilty after he was caught. Neither of them denied what they'd done to her."

Alicia didn't say anything. But what could she say? He'd barred her from another "I'm sorry."

She fidgeted with her hands, a sign that she wanted to escape the situation she was in. This was making her as uncomfortable as it made him. But it didn't take a behavioral analyst to figure that out. Anyone could've seen it, if anyone else had been around.

"It's on the Internet," he said.

"What?"

"The murder. If you Google my name, it'll come up. There isn't a lot of information. Mostly it's newspaper articles from when it first happened. Most of the crime-scene details were withheld, so it wasn't sensational-ized. But it's still out there that my wife was killed in a home invasion robbery."

More fidgeting. "So you've been keeping a secret from me that isn't really a secret?"

"Yes, but it wasn't something I'd planned to discuss with you. I realize that it might seem as if I'm not han-dling my loss very well, but I've had plenty of grief counseling. I've talked about the murder at great length."

But that was what he did best. He focused on death. It was the living part that was difficult for him. "It hasn't affected my ability to do my job."

She went philosophical, hitting much too close to the mark. "There's more to a person than his or her job."

"I know, but between my work and my daughter, there isn't time for anything else."

"You found time to be alone with me on a private island." She made a wide gesture, as if showcasing the beach. "But it's turning into a strange kind of paradise, isn't it?" Her hands floated back to her lap. "I want to hold you. I want to show you how sorry I am for what happened to Katie, but I'm afraid you'll reject my com-passion."

"Truthfully, I would. Now isn't the time for me to be held." If he let her get too close, if he allowed her to break through his defense mechanism, it would weaken him.

She gazed at the stretch of sand. "Now isn't the time to build a castle, either."

"No, I suppose it isn't." He wasn't in the mood to feign a fairy tale.

They both stood up and carried the supplies back to the SUV. But before they climbed into the vehicle, she said, "Will you at least comfort me, Griffin?"

Christ, he thought. There was no way out of this. She wasn't being clever. Unbridled honesty was evident in her eyes.

He walked forward and wrapped her in his arms. She clung to him, and he knew he would remember, as well as regret, this moment for the rest of his life. She felt soft and insecure, vulnerable in a way he could barely describe. Had he made a mistake in taking her on a romantic getaway? Had he pushed the boundaries of their affair into another realm?

In some small way, he was taking comfort from her, too. And it hurt, damn it. It hurt more with each second that ticked by.

Griffin nuzzled Alicia's hair, breathing her in like a wounded wolf. "This trip was supposed to be about sex."

"I know." She kept her cheek against his chest. "But I'm not feeling very sexual right now." She lifted her head a fraction. "Are you?"

"No." But he wished that he were. When they were in the throes of passion, the eroticism blocked his pain.

She remained in his arms, keeping her body close to his. Her heart, too. He could feel the emotion-laced beats.

The time they had left together was diminishing, and even after what he'd put her through today, he could tell that she didn't want it to end.

But they both knew that their affair wasn't destined to last, so he didn't warn her about longing for more. He figured she'd already been warning herself, and she didn't need to be cautioned by the know-it-all profiler.

So, as he held her a little tighter, he turned the caution on himself. Keeping her wasn't an option. In less than two weeks, he was going to let Alicia Greco go.

And do his damnedest not to look back.

Returning to the mainland was surreal.

Alicia and Griffin entered their adjoining hotel rooms and unpacked their overnight bags. She glanced at her lover, but he seemed preoccupied.

"I've got a meeting with Inoke," he said.

"Now?"

He nodded. "The memorial is tomorrow. I need to check on the final arrangements."

The G-man was back, she thought. Of course, there was more to Griffin than being a government operative. He'd lost his wife to a murder. Although the subject hadn't resurfaced, Katie Malone weighed heavily on Alicia's mind.

He buttoned himself into a crisp white shirt and put a perfect knot in his slim black tie. His gun was holstered to his belt.

"I'll see you later." He came forward and gave her a quick peck.

To her, it was the type of kiss a work-bound husband would give his stay-at-home wife, and Alicia wondered if Griffin used to kiss Katie that way when he hurried out the door.

A second later, he appeared to realize what he'd done. Apparently it struck a déjà-vu vibe. He stalled and skimmed Alicia's check, as if he had the sudden urge to stay. But he didn't. He stepped back and left her alone, taking his briefcase and laptop with him.

She gazed at the empty surroundings. Maybe she should focus on her job, too. Maybe that would keep her mind off of Griffin…and his wife.

She leafed through her notes and examined the Secret Traveler checklist of the hotel's activities and amenities. She'd lucked out when she'd received this assignment, being afforded ample time to rate the resort. Of course, finding bodies on the beach wasn't lucking out. And neither was getting heartsick over the profiler.

Anxious to keep busy, she returned to the checklist and decided to visit the business center. The Siga Resort boasted about their high-speed Internet connection in their brochure, so she might as well test their claim.

And do what? a small voice inside her asked. Google Griffin's name and read about his wife's murder?

No, another voice responded. *No.* She would steer clear of that.

Determined to prove her professionalism, she walked to the hotel lobby and entered the business center. It offered twenty-four-hour service with four computer workstations, color printers, several copy machines, pens, paper, staplers and other office essentials.

She secured a workstation and sat down to surf the Net. But after she got online, she stalled. Her fingers itched to type *Special Agent Griffin Malone* in the subject search. But she didn't do it.

In a frazzled instant, she typed *The Sex on the Beach Killer* instead.

Zoom. The high-speed connection lived up to the claim. Link after link appeared. Alicia started clicking on them, scanning the contents. The article in that day's *Fiji Times* appeared, and she read it. The upcoming memorial was featured with pictures of Paxton and Veronica from their final modeling assignment, photos that had become part of their obituary rather than glossing the pages of a fashion magazine.

A few more clicks and she came across pictures of the other victims, the other couples the Sex on the Beach Killer had slashed.

For the next thirty to forty minutes, Alicia continued the search. She read articles that mentioned her own name, identifying her as the tourist who'd discovered Veronica and Paxton's bodies. As for Griffin, his name appeared here and there, as did Inspector Inoke's, both names attached to quotes from press release statements.

She knew that she should quit before she went too far, walk away from the Internet and focus on other aspects of the business center. But the urge to Google Griffin's name by itself wrapped its ugly hands around her.

Tap. Tap. Tap.

She typed in *Special Agent Griffin Malone.*

Zip. Zip. Zip.

The Sex on the Beach articles in which he'd been quoted appeared again, but she skipped past those.

She discovered that FBI profilers didn't draw a lot of media attention, not unless they'd retired from the Bureau and had documented their careers in bestselling books or TV shows.

Griffin had been right. His wife's murder hadn't been sensationalized. She found the newspaper write-ups he'd told her about. The articles were factual, but with very little detail. Nowhere was it cited that the victim had been bound and gagged or crammed into a closet. Apparently the FBI had done a thorough job of keeping the crime scene under wraps.

All Alicia learned that she didn't already know was that Katie Malone had been thirty-eight years old when she'd died. Alicia kept searching, hoping to come across a picture of Katie, but she didn't find one.

She clicked on the final link—an old interview Griffin had granted the press. He talked about the men who'd shot his wife and commended the police for apprehending them so quickly. That was it. That was what he gave the media, and it seemed to satisfy them. The profiler was off the hook. His name hadn't become synonymous with his wife's murder. But a random home invasion robbery wasn't shattering news, especially when the offenders were behind bars and the special agent was grounded enough to continue his job.

If they only knew how tortured he really was, she thought. Then again, maybe they wouldn't care about his grief. The press was more interested in the psychopaths he profiled. Men like the Sex on the Beach Killer were the newsmakers. Griffin was just part of the law enforcement mix.

But not to Alicia. She moved the mouse to the *X* at the top right-hand corner and closed the display, getting off the Internet.

To her, he was so much more.

Alicia and Griffin didn't make love that night. They slept beside each other in the same bed, but they barely talked, let alone touched and kissed. She didn't tell him that she'd looked him up on the Internet, and he didn't second-guess her. But his mind was elsewhere. He was preoccupied with the memorial.

In the morning, Alicia stressed over the public event.

"Are you sure you're up to this?" he asked.

She nodded. They were already dressed and ready, but they weren't attending the memorial together. In fact, Griffin wasn't going at all. He and Inspector Inoke would be viewing the happenings from security monitors set up in another room at the hotel, where they would communicate with undercover officers at the beach. Alicia would be sporting an audio device so she could communicate with Griffin and Inspector Inoke, too. That way, she could alert them quickly if she saw the man from the disco.

When she'd volunteered to help, she hadn't considered anything like this. She'd assumed that Griffin would be there with her in person. But she wasn't about to back out of the deal.

"Don't give any interviews to the press," he said.

"I won't." The last thing she wanted to do was talk to reporters. "Do you think it's going to be a circus?"

"It'll be crowded, but we're hoping for a calm turn-out." He studied her. "Are you ready to go?"

She nodded. She knew he meant to the other room for her audio device.

He moved closer. "One kiss before we head out?"

"Yes." Please, yes. She needed to draw from his strength, to hold him close. She'd missed being intimate with him last night.

He slanted his mouth over hers, and she tasted the warmth of his lips. How in God's name was she going to keep herself from falling in love with him?

Very cautiously, she thought.

When they drifted apart, she looked into his haunted blue eyes. Today, they were as vivid as a sapphire sea. "Don't analyze me anymore, Griffin. Don't second-guess what I'm thinking or feeling."

He frowned. "All I did was kiss you."

"I know. But sometimes you start delving into my mind. And I'd prefer to keep my emotions to myself."

"Most of the time, you wear your emotions on your sleeve. But I'll quit doing it." He toyed with a strand of her hair. "You look pretty today."

Smooth transition, she thought. He'd changed the subject without so much as a blink. "Thank you." Because the memorial was on the beach and mourners had been encouraged to wear casual attire, she'd chosen a simple summer dress and sandals. Her hair—the object of his fascination—was long and loose and decorated with a seashell comb.

"Are Veronica's and Paxton's families going to be there?" she asked.

"No. They returned to the States to make their own arrangements. But some of Veronica's and Paxton's friends will be in attendance."

"And a lot of strangers, too, I would imagine."

He nodded. "That's why this is being held publicly. To see what strangers show up."

"Yes, of course." The authorities were hoping to catch the killer on videotape, whoever he might be. Some of the undercover cops would be posing as cameramen so they could record the mourners.

Griffin escorted Alicia to a room at the end of their hotel block, and the moment they entered, her anxiety level kicked up a notch.

Inspector Inoke and various other cops were seated in front of monitors that were already active. Apparently the cameramen cops were in place and doing their jobs.

Alicia gazed at one of the screens. She could see the beach and the floral-draped structure that had been built for the memorial. It was a little bigger than the original cabana, with a pulpit in the center for the spiritual leaders who were scheduled to speak. For now, a row of uniformed policemen guarded it. The service was an hour away, but people had begun to gather on the sand.

"Anything?" Griffin asked Inoke.

The inspector shook his head. "No one who fits the profile."

A female officer came forward, and Griffin introduced Alicia to her and moved out of the way. The other woman fiddled with the bodice of Alicia's dress and fitted her with a concealed microphone. A tiny receiver for the inside of her ear canal came next. The lady cop explained how the device worked, and they tested it. The process was simple, like using an invisible Bluetooth.

"Now what?" Alicia asked Griffin.

"Just stay here until the time gets closer."

She wanted him to kiss her again, but she knew he wouldn't show her affection in front of the police.

So Alicia took a seat and waited to embark on the memorial, to recite prayers for the deceased and scan the faces of other attendees.

Anxious, she kept glancing at her watch. Of course that made her wait seem even longer. But as the minutes passed, more and more people gathered on the beach. She could see them on the monitor Griffin was viewing.

When he told her it was time for her to go, she was ready. She couldn't take another moment of feeling out of place, of being with Griffin yet not being with him.

He walked her to the door, and they exchanged a few brief words. In this setting, he was all FBI.

Alicia ventured outside, took the stairs and headed toward the memorial site. Of course she wasn't the only resort guest walking in that direction. The crowd was thickening. She tested her audio device once again, just to be sure, and it was working just fine.

A few minutes later, several off-duty hotel employees on their way to the service glanced her way and said, *"Bula,"* which meant hello in Fijian. She returned the greeting.

Alicia reached her destination and walked through the crowd, looking for the man from the disco, if he decided to make an appearance. The mourners were an eclectic mix, but Fiji was a multiracial, multicultured nation. Voices buzzed. She heard British, Australian and American accents, along with Fijian and Hindi sounds.

She noticed a tall, strikingly handsome man in loose-fitting shorts, a short-sleeve shirt and bare feet. He looked like a surfer. Or a model. She wondered if were a friend of Paxton's, or maybe a former lover of Veronica's.

There were a lot of attractive people. A stunning red-head in an ankle-length dress was fingering a rosary bead necklace. Beside her was a pretty blonde in a stylish straw hat and designer sunglasses.

Of course there were average folk, too—all walks of life. A recognizable reporter from an American news station glanced Alicia's way, and she dodged out of sight, weaving into the middle of the pack, still searching for the possible killer. But she felt as if she were looking for a warped needle in a haystack.

The service began, and the crowd hushed. The overwhelming quiet cut through Alicia like a knife. She pushed away a gruesome image of Paxton and Veronica in the cabana and said a silent prayer for them instead.

Christian, Muslim, Sikh and Hindu spiritual leaders took turns speaking. A host of Fijian chiefs from nearby villages offered condolences, too. They paid respect to all of the victims who'd been murdered, whose lives had been taken needlessly.

Hundreds of flowers circulated through the assemblage. Someone handed Alicia a fuchsia-colored bloom.

The ceremony wound down with mourners tossing their flowers into the ocean. Alicia followed suit, saying goodbye to Veronica and Paxton, young lovers she never even knew. She added a silent prayer for the other victims, too.

As she watched the tide come in and take the flowers out to sea, she walked along the shore and scanned the retreating crowd. When she got an ominous feeling that the killer was searching for her, too, she hoped it was her imagination at work.

That there was nothing to fear except for her overactive mind.

Chapter 8

Alicia waited in the dark with the covers drawn tight. The entire day and most of the night had passed, and Griffin was still working. But she'd expected as much. After the memorial, she'd gone back to the monitor room, and he'd told her that he would be late, that he and Inspector Inoke would be viewing all of the video footage, frame by frame.

At that point she'd felt silly for feeling as if the killer had been there, looking specifically for her, especially since she hadn't seen the man from the disco or anyone else who'd seemed suspicious. So she hadn't mentioned it to Griffin.

But now she realized that she should have. Just to be honest. Just to let him know where her scrambled head was at.

A noise caught her attention, and she sat up. Surely it was Griffin returning to their shared accommodations. He always entered through his own room, then joined her in hers. She turned on the nightlight above her bed and waited for him.

About ten minutes later, he appeared, stripped down to his boxer-briefs. Alicia was wearing an oversized T-shirt and skimpy panties.

"I'd thought you'd be asleep by now," he said.

"I sleep better when you're here. But I'm sure I'll go back to my normal sleeping habits when I get home," she added, trying to sound less dependent on him.

He got into bed and leaned forward to kiss her, not a sensual kiss, but not a peck, either. It was somewhere in between. He tasted spearmint-fresh, like the toothpaste he'd just used. She savored the flavor. Everything about him enticed her.

He let go, then said, "What a day," with frustration evident in his voice.

She probed him about the memorial. "I guess it's safe to assume that there wasn't anyone who sparked your interest?"

"No, but it's not a simple task, picking a possible killer out of a crowd. We're going to go over the footage again, as many times as we have to, just in case we missed something."

Alicia shifted her legs, trying to get comfortable, and the sheet billowed between them. "I should have told you this earlier, but during the end of the service, I got a little scared." She explained the ominous feeling she'd gotten at the beach. "I'm sure it was just my imagination. You know how creeped out I get by all of this."

He studied her in that profiler way of his. Deeply. Intently. She resisted the uncomfortable urge to squirm.

"Don't ever keep things from me," he said. "Not things that make you afraid."

"I won't. But now you're spooking me even more."

"I'm sorry. I don't mean to. But it's important for you to feel safe." Shadows from the overhead light sharpened his features. "I don't want you involved in this case anymore."

"Because I scare so easily? I've been like that since the beginning. Remember how I thought the killer was running after me when I was jogging?"

"Yeah, and now those fears are coming back. You're too caught up in this, Alicia. It isn't good for you."

Being on the verge of falling in love with him wasn't good for her, either. "No more hypnosis? No more looking for the man from the disco?"

"No. I should have kept you out of it all along."

"How could you? I'm the girl who found the bodies. The same girl who watched the victims dance. And who might have seen the killer. I'm the best witness you've got."

"And the most afraid." He tugged her closer. Kissable close. But he didn't put his mouth against hers. "It makes me worry about you."

"I'm fine, Griffin." Especially now that she was snuggled in his arms. "You don't need to worry about me. I've always had an overactive imagination. When I was little, I used to check under my bed for Gila monsters."

He tilted his head. "In a suburb in Illinois?"

"I just said that I had an overactive imagination."

"I hope you're not afraid of geckos. They're all over

Fiji. There might even be one lurking around. Do you want me to check?"

She smiled at his genuine concern. "I'm over the lizard thing. Besides, when I was in elementary school, the other kids used to call me Alicia *Gecko* instead of Alicia *Greco*."

"That was your nickname?"

"Yes, it was. And I learned to embrace it."

"Sure you did. If a gecko darted out from under the bed, you know damn well you'd be screeching like a teakettle."

"Not if it was the cute little guy from those TV commercials."

He raised his eyebrows. "The car insurance spokesman?"

They both laughed, but a second later, he tightened his hold on her, remaining protective.

They separated, and she asked, "What type of kid were you?"

"Sometimes I goofed off, but mostly I got good grades and worked hard to achieve my goals. I was analytical, but I was a creative thinker, too."

Like now, she thought.

He continued, "In high school, I ran cross-country, and competed on a junior rifle team. My mom wasn't too thrilled about the gun club at first. She argued with my dad about it, but later she was my biggest supporter. She attended every match. My sisters, too."

"You have sisters?"

"Two. Betty and Bonnie. Otherwise known as bossy and bossier." He smiled with obvious affection. "They're older and supposedly wiser than I am."

"What do they do now?"

"Bonnie is in real estate, and Betty is a pastor's wife. I think she married him to repent for hitting me with that big ol' Bible she used to tote around."

Alicia caught the mischief in his voice. "You're making this up."

"All right, so it might have been a dictionary or a thesaurus or some other monstrous book. But she did smack me with it." He rubbed the top of his head as if he still bore a bump. "She got mad because I called her Betty Boobs when she got her first training bra."

"Then I'd say you had it coming."

He defended his kid-self. "Bonnie dared me to do it. She was the instigator."

"And you were the innocent little brother?" She enjoyed being curled up in bed with him, listening to his animated stories. "I'm an only child, but I always wanted brothers and sisters. Our house was loving, but it was quiet."

"I know. I can tell." He winced. "Sorry. I just did what I'm not supposed to do."

"Break the rules and analyze me? It's okay. My parents have been together for thirty-one years. That's something to be proud of." She envisioned her folks in their Norman Rockwell lives. "They were my role models for marriage before my 'I do' with Jimmy failed. Now I think my parents are a rare breed."

"Mine, too. Their fiftieth anniversary is coming up. The golden milestone. My sisters are already planning the party." He searched her gaze. "I really am sorry."

"For not being able to control your urge to analyze me?" She skimmed his stomach. He had yummy abs.

"How can I hold it against you? Especially since you offered to slay a dragon for me."

"There you go with that imagination of yours." He rolled over on top of her, pinning her in place. "It was an itty-bitty gecko, and I never said I'd slay it."

"Oh, that's right." She batted her lashes, behaving like a princess in distress. Or maybe she was mimicking a Southern belle. She'd never been an accomplished actress.

Griffin didn't tease her back. Apparently he was ready to get serious. He lowered his head, intent on kissing her deep and slow, and as his mouth claimed hers, she lost all sense of reason. The only thing that mattered was being with her lover.

And taking the intimacy he was willing to give.

Two days later, Alicia was alone in her room, going through her work notes.

A rap sounded on the door, followed by a feminine voice that announced, "Hotel delivery."

She got up from her seat to answer the summons, and the employee handed her a letter-size envelope.

"This arrived for you in the mail," the other woman said.

"Thank you." Alicia was glad it wasn't a freebie from the hotel. From time to time, she and Griffin were still getting complimentary vouchers that they never used.

After the delivery girl left, she examined the envelope before tearing it open. It was addressed to her, care of the Siga Hotel and Resort. There was no return address, but it had been postmarked in the Republic of Fiji. Obviously, it was a local correspondence. She assumed it was from Zoë or Madeline.

But she was wrong.

The letter opened with *Dear Ms. Greco.*

That certainly wasn't the way either of her friends would have referred to her.

She kept reading.

I looked for you the other day, but I didn't see you. Were you there? At the memorial?

Alicia sat on the edge of the bed, her hands threatening to tremble.

I didn't attend the service. I watched portions of it on the news. It was quite a show. I wish they had broadcast it in its entirety.

But I'm getting ahead of myself, so I'll start over. I know you found the bodies. I read your name in the paper, and I saw you being interviewed on TV the day after that disgusting couple got what they deserved.

Alicia held her breath. Was this the killer? Was this *him?*

I'll bet you're wondering who I am.

A choked sound escaped her lips.

Maybe you should ask Special Agent Malone who he thinks I am. It's exciting, isn't it? That they brought an FBI profiler all the way to the South Pacific?

Griffin…Griffin…Griffin. Alicia whispered her lover's name in her mind.

So, what did it feel like to find the bodies? Was it exhilarating? Did you picture the knife entering their exposed flesh? Tearing into them with razor-sharp force?

I so love a bloodbath, don't you? But only when sinners are begging to be cleansed. I'm not a violent person by nature.

I'll write to you again, and next time, I'll tell you a bit more about myself. Surely, Agent Malone would like that. He must be working hard to figure me out.

Oops! Did I just give away my identity?

As the letter concluded, the tone changed to one of eerie politeness.

Have a nice day, Ms. Greco. And, please, give the profiler my regards.

Alicia let go of the letter and dashed to the phone, dialing Griffin's cell.

By the third ring, she was ready to scream. If he didn't answer—

"Malone."

"Oh, God, Griffin, the killer wrote to me. The hotel delivered a letter, and I just read it and…"

He went right into being an agent…and a lover. "Stay there. Stay with me on the phone. Don't hang up. I'm on my way."

"Okay." She latched on to his voice like a lifeline. "He

mentioned you in the letter, too. I dropped it on the floor. I don't want to pick it up again." All she wanted to do right now was fling her arms around her G-man.

Then she would be all right. Then she would be strong. She could hear him handling the situation from his end.

"A uniformed officer who's already in the area should arrive before I do. He's going to stay outside your door until I get there. Inoke is off today, but he's being notified as we speak."

"That all sounds fine to me." Especially since Griffin was going to stay on the line with her, the way a 9-1-1 operator would do with an emergency caller.

Within a short time, Griffin told her to check the peephole on her door. She peered through the scope and saw the officer he'd dispatched. Apparently Griffin was in radio communication with the police while he was on the phone with her.

She breathed a little easier.

Finally the special agent showed up and entered her room, dismissing the uniformed cop.

"I'm so glad to see you." Alicia wrapped her arms around Griffin's neck.

"Inoke is on his way. But it'll be a while before he gets here. For now, it's just you and me."

That worked for her. He held her close, and everything about him felt familiar, from his woodsy scent to his perfectly knotted tie to the breadth of his shoulders. But the hug ended too soon.

"Where's the letter?" he asked.

"There." She pointed the spot where she'd dropped it.

"And the envelope is over there." She gestured to the dining table.

Griffin reached into his pocket and removed a pair of latex gloves. Alicia watched him, feeling as if she were in the middle of a CSI nightmare.

She didn't know what to do, whether to sit, to cross her arms, to walk onto the veranda and get some fresh air. She'd never been so aware of herself, of her environment. Her mind was racing, and her pulse was running to catch up.

She studied Griffin as he read the correspondence, but his expression was inscrutable. Alicia didn't want to be afraid; she didn't want to let the killer take control of her.

The waiting seemed to go on forever. Griffin was reading the letter for a second time, then a third. She considered making a midday pot of coffee, but caffeine wouldn't help. It would only make her more jumpy. Decaffeinated, then? Or maybe a cup of herbal tea?

Griffin looked up at her, and she forgot about a hot drink. There it was. His expression. His eyes were more haunted than usual. Or maybe they were just catching a ghostly ray of light from the window.

"Whoever wrote this appears to fit the profile, to share the offender's views. He's smart and clever, and he's truly interested in how you felt when you found the bodies. But mostly, he wrote to you to get my attention, to make a bigger impact on the profiler. But none of those things identifies him as the killer, not for certain."

"But it *has* to be from him. Who else would go to such extremes?"

"A lot of people." Griffin spoke gently. "False confessions and communiqués—letters, poems, phone calls—

are extremely common, especially in high-profile cases. Media-addicted and/or mentally ill persons often crave credit for heinous acts they didn't commit. And sometimes they're pretty darn convincing."

To her, that wasn't good enough. Alicia wanted definite answers. "What's he supposed to say that identifies him as the real killer?"

"I'm sorry, but I can't discuss that with you. It's something only the offender and law enforcement know."

He placed the letter and envelope in an evidence bag he'd brought with him and set it on the table. Then he removed his gloves and came toward her.

Would they find fingerprints on the letter? she wondered. Or DNA on the envelope? Or anything useful?

He made a tight expression. "I'm sorry you've been put in this position. That whoever he is, he chose to write to you instead of making direct contact with me or the police. This is the last thing in the world I want to happen to you."

"To be caught up in some crazy person's game? To wait around for his next correspondence to find out if he's the real killer?" She glanced at the evidence bag. "Are you going to give a copy of the letter to your BAU team in the States?"

He nodded. "I'll analyze it with them. We'll go over every single word. And I'll discuss it in depth with Inoke, too."

"It wasn't my imagination that someone was looking for me at the memorial. Only he was searching for me on TV." She fought a shiver. "How strange is that?"

"You weren't supposed to be involved anymore. You and I settled that. We agreed that you'd be free of this."

His voice went rough. "Damn it all to hell." He took her in his arms.

"I'll be okay if I'm with you." She put her head on his shoulder. "You're the FBI. What could be safer than that? So don't you dare tell me to go home early."

"I wasn't. Not until I know who wrote to you and what he wants." Griffin's grip got more protective. "I can't be with you every second of the day, but I'll still make sure that you're safe. I swear I will." Another tight hold. "I'll talk to Inoke about providing protection for you when I'm not around. If he can't spare a man, then I'll talk to the Bureau about sending another agent. If they can't get someone here soon enough, I'll get my friend's security company involved."

"Thank you." Going home this soon wasn't an option. She needed her G-man.

The fear of falling in love zoomed into focus, then went blurry, making her wish, for the millionth time, that she wasn't having those types of feelings about him.

Determined to lighten her own mood, to keep their affair in perspective, she stepped back and said, "If you're going to provide me with a part-time cop or agent or bodyguard, do you think I could have a guy who looks like Tom Laruso?"

He gave her a quizzical look. "The pilot? The man you've got in mind for Madeline?"

"Yes, but I like him, too." She flashed a deliberate grin. "He's one hot ticket. Oh, wait. So are you. So I guess one hottie is enough."

His eyebrows winged, but now he was smiling, too. "I should hope so."

Grateful her diversion had worked, she broadened her

grin. "What do you think, Agent McSafety? Should we go for a quickie before Inspector Inoke gets here?"

"He's too good a cop. He would know exactly what we did." But damned if Griffin didn't look tempted.

Knock. Knock.

Right on cue, Inoke announced himself on the other side of the door.

And with him came the reminder of the serial killer letter, whether genuine or not, that had been addressed to Alicia.

As the sun melded into the ocean, painting vivid colors across the sky, Griffin turned to look at Alicia. They were alone on her veranda, seated in wrought-iron chairs. Inoke had come and gone, and the evening was wearing on.

Griffin was doing his damnedest to stay objective, to stop his personal feelings from getting in the way, but he wanted to bang his head against the railing for being so damn remiss.

Why hadn't he seen this coming? Why hadn't he predicted that Alicia might be the subject of a communiqué?

The letter didn't appear to be a direct threat, but Griffin wasn't about to take it at face value. And, luckily, neither was Inspector Inoke. He'd agreed that Alicia should be provided with police protection when Griffin wasn't by her side, so at least that was in the works.

"First thing tomorrow you and I are going to talk to the hotel manager," he said.

"Why?"

"To discuss security measures with him. If another letter arrives, I don't want the hotel to deliver it to you. I want them to notify me immediately. I want you to tell the hotel manager who you are, too. That you work for the Secret Traveler. This is a security issue now, and he and his security team should be privy to your true identity."

"I understand," she said.

Between the overwhelming need to keep Alicia safe and the horror from Griffin's past, he was twisted into complicated knots. He kept seeing flashes of Katie in his mind: the duct tape over her mouth, the bullet hole in her chest, the crimson stain soaking her blouse.

"Will you give me details about the killer?" Alicia asked, redirecting his tormented focus. "Or at least everything you're allowed to discuss? No matter who wrote that letter, I want to know more about the killer."

He understood how she felt. Knowledge was power, and she was trying to gain control over the situation she was in. "First of all, his crime scenes are a mixed presentation."

"I don't understand what that means."

"For example, leaving bodies at the death scene and in plain view is considered disorganized, but the weapon being absent is organized. He targets strangers. That's organized, too. Of course, it's a lot more complex than that, but those are the types of things taken into account."

Alicia scooted to the edge of her seat, clearly waiting for more information.

Griffin obliged. "Personality-wise, an organized offender is socially competent and intelligent. Following his crimes in the media is another aspect of being organized."

"All of which this guy exhibits."

"He also experienced harsh discipline during childhood, is anxious when he commits his crimes, lives alone rather than with a partner and is sexually incompetent."

"I gather those fall into the disorganized category."

"Yes, they do." And he wished that he and Alicia weren't having this conversation. That she'd never come to Fiji, never found the bodies and never slept with him. But it was too late to turn back the clock.

"You can certainly tell a lot about someone from his actions, can't you?" She sat back in her chair. "What *exactly* does sexually incompetent mean?"

"It's a general term. But in this case, it means he's incapable of experiencing intimacy, emotionally and physically."

"So, he's a nutcase who can't get it up?"

Griffin almost smiled. Alicia had a way about her. "You could say that. His impotence is a psychological condition. He can't get an erection because his mind won't let him."

"Does he resent men and women equally? To me, he seems to hate women more." She reached up to touch her own neck. "The way he slashed Veronica's throat—it seemed harsher than what he did to Paxton."

The urge to smile vanished. "It was. He punishes his female victims more than their male counterparts. He believes that women are capable of poisoning men's minds. But men who allow themselves to be poisoned deserve to be punished, too. Of course he's taking a chance by targeting couples."

Alicia lowered her hand, slowly, methodically. "With men who are strong enough to fight back?"

"Yes, but being engaged in sex makes them unaware. Most of the time, the men don't know what hit them until it's too late."

She glanced out at the sea, where dusk was falling into shadows. "What an MO."

"Actually, everything in his behavior isn't his MO. Some of it is his signature." Griffin explained the difference and gazed at the darkening ocean view. "MO is the way an offender goes about committing his crimes, and signature is something that's associated with why he does it. It's what gives him emotional satisfaction. But sometimes there's a fine line between the two."

"You told me that safe, sexy men were my MO."

"I used MO because I assumed you'd be familiar with the term, and in a noncriminal sense it's used to describe someone's habits."

"Can MOs be changed?"

He nodded. "Criminals often change their MOs. But their signatures always stay the same."

She made a worried face. "Then my MO feels more like a signature to me."

Griffin wasn't about to respond. He didn't want to think too deeply about the reason Alicia had gotten attached to him so quickly or why he was struggling with his feelings. Not when he needed to channel his energy into keeping her safe.

The very thing he'd failed to do for his wife.

Chapter 9

The hotel manager, Robert Lomu, looked as if he'd just lost a billion bucks and didn't have another copper penny to his highly respected name.

Well, okay, maybe he didn't look *that* bad. But this had to be one of the worst professional days of his life.

Alicia noticed that Robert's tropical complexion lacked its usual luster, and his receding hairline seemed to be moving farther back on his head.

And why not? Alicia and Griffin, the guests he'd been trying so hard to impress, were seated in his office with distressing news. He'd just learned about the letter. And to top it off, Alicia had come clean about her job. So now he knew that the tourist who'd found the bodies and received a suspicious letter was also the Secret Traveler evaluator who'd been assigned to the hotel.

"None of this will affect my rating," Alicia assured him.

"But how impartial can you be?" Robert asked in his polished British accent. "Surely you must be anxious to leave this experience behind."

"Not all of it. I'm enjoying the hotel and resort." Besides, she had Robert to thank for putting Griffin in the room next to hers, for making the special agent more accessible. Of course, that wasn't something she dared mention out loud.

The manager seemed to relax. His shoulders weren't quite so rigid anymore. He turned his gaze on Griffin. "Naturally, we'll cooperate with your investigation. Whatever is required of us, we'll be at your disposal."

In response, Griffin explained that if anything arrived for Alicia with her name or room number on it, management needed to contact him immediately. "Another letter, flowers, balloons, singing telegrams," he said. "No matter what it is, notify me instead of allowing it to be delivered. Also, the police are going to forward any calls that come in for Ms. Greco through your switchboard to another number."

"I understand." Robert folded his hands on his desk. "Is there anything else?"

"I'd like to meet with your security staff and discuss all of this with them." Griffin glanced at his watch. "But Inspector Inoke won't be available until noon, and he needs to be present at the meeting, too."

"No problem. We'll arrange it at the inspector's convenience. He knows our security staff quite well."

After Griffin thanked the hotel manager, he and Alicia left Robert's office and walked through the lobby. From there, they headed outside and into the morning sun.

"So, where are my calls going to be forwarded?" she asked.

He reached for his sunglasses, but he didn't put them on. "To a satellite phone."

"And who's going to be in possession of that phone?"

"A female cop, the one who fitted you with the audio device for the memorial. Do you remember her?"

Alicia nodded, recalling the other woman's strong but personable nature. "Officer Mol…something or other."

"Molias. Besides manning your calls, she's going to be your police protection."

"For when you're not around? Really? Inoke chose a woman for the job?" She angled her head, studying him in the daylight. "Or was that your idea?"

"Because of your wisecrack about wanting a body-guard who looks like the 'hot-ticket' pilot? No, that didn't have anything to do with it."

She teased him. "And here I pegged you for the jealous type."

"Maybe a little." He laughed it off. "But Inoke picked Molias. And I'm pleased with his choice. She's an ex-ceptional cop."

"You don't really think I'm going to receive flowers or balloons?" She hesitated. "Or a singing telegram?"

"No, but I want the hotel to be prepared for anything."

Alicia couldn't stop herself from making a bad joke. "A guy in a gorilla suit? A bad Elvis impersonator?"

"Now that you put it like that." He caught the corner of her eye, and they both laughed—really laughed.

A second later, they went completely silent.

Trapped in the absurdity of life. And the uncertainty that always seemed to go with it.

* * *

Alicia spent the second part of the day with Officer Molias. The other woman, dressed in casual clothes, blended into the background while Alicia worked.

At dinnertime, Griffin was still with Inspector Inoke, and Alicia was still with Officer Molias, so they dined at a seafood restaurant in Suva instead of staying at the resort.

It was the largest city in Oceania, the capitol of Fiji and the only place in the island chain with high-rise buildings. There was no beach in Suva and the weather wasn't as sunny, but it pulsed with activity.

The municipal market, with its street vendors and *yaqona* dens, fascinated Alicia. *Yaqona,* more commonly known as *kava,* was a tongue-numbing, tranquilizing, nonalcoholic drink made from the dried roots of pepper plants.

"You can call me Nalani," the female officer said. "That's my given name."

"It's beautiful," Alicia responded, as they sat across from each other with a view of the port. "Does it have a Fijian meaning?"

"It's not Fijian. It's Hawaiian. I was born there, so my family gave me a Hawaiian name. It means calmness of the skies." Tall, with strong-boned features and curly, dark hair fashioned in a simple twist, Nalani was uniquely attractive. "I like your name, too. What does it mean?"

"Noble." But Alicia thought that Nalani looked like the noble one. "It's the Latin form of Alice."

"What about your surname?"

"It's Italian, but it means someone who originates from Greece."

"In Fiji, some people don't have surnames, and some have two given names, one Christian and one traditional. Sometimes we are known by different names at different stages of our lives."

"I love Fiji," Alicia remarked. "I'll be sorry when it's time for me to leave."

"Even with what's been going on?"

"Yes. That sounds crazy, doesn't it?"

"Not when there's a man involved."

Alicia paused in the middle of eating, a prawn halfway to her mouth. Apparently Inspector Inoke wasn't the only cop who'd figured things out. "Are my feelings for Griffin that obvious?"

"Yes, but he has obvious affection for you, too. I remember what those early tingles were like. My husband used to look at me the way the agent looks at you." A sly smile spread across Nalani's face. "Sometimes he still does."

What could she say? First Zoë compared her relationship with Breeze to what Alicia was feeling for Griffin, and now Nalani was on the same track.

"What does your husband do?" Alicia asked, changing the subject.

"He owns an auto mechanic shop. But he works with youth groups, too. He's a good man." The other woman scooped some rice onto her fork. "We have two children, a son and a daughter. Timothy is six, and Teresa is four."

"Who watches them when you and your husband are working?"

"My mother. We live in the town where we were raised. Near our families." Nalani glanced toward the door as a group of tourists entered the eatery, then turned her attention back to the conversation. "It would be nice if you and Agent Malone could come to our house before you leave Fiji. We would enjoy having you as our guests."

Alicia considered the invitation. No matter how much she tried to deny it, the picture Nalani painted sounded nice. Very nice. "I'd enjoy it, too."

"Then you'll ask the agent?"

"Yes, I'll ask him."

Nalani seemed pleased, and Alicia wondered how Griffin was going to react to her and the policewoman making "girly" plans.

They continued to chat, and soon the waiter cleared their plates and brought them each a bowl of banana pudding for dessert.

At the moment, it didn't even seem as if Alicia was under police protection, but she wouldn't be in the company of a cop if the possibility of danger didn't exist.

Griffin waited for Alicia to get home. *Home?* The rooms they shared weren't home. That wasn't a word that fit this scenario.

He walked over to the minibar and poured himself some seltzer water. He knew that Alicia was having dinner. Officer Molias had been keeping him informed of their whereabouts.

He sipped his drink, put the glass on the bar top and glanced at his watch, anxious for Alicia to return.

By the time she arrived, he'd shucked his suit and was dressed in sweatpants and an FBI T-shirt.

"How'd it go?" he asked.

"With Nalani?" Alicia changed into loungewear, too,

only her T-shirt had a picture of Humphrey Bogart and Ingrid Bergman on it. "I really like her."

"Nalani, huh? Not Officer Molias? Sounds like you two bonded." Not that he was surprised. Women sometimes told each other their life stories while waiting in line at Wal-Mart, let alone sitting down together for dinner.

"Yes, we did. In fact, she invited us to her house to meet her family."

He went from looking at the *Casablanca* image on her top to fighting an ache in his chest. He almost felt as if he were married again. Katie used to orchestrate get-togethers. "When?"

"Whenever we have time. I realize it might not be possible, but it sounded like a nice idea." She proceeded to tell him what she knew about Molias and her husband and their children.

"That's fine. We'll try to do it." Especially if Alicia needed the diversion.

Or was he agreeing for himself? Was he drawn to the family life she'd just described? To someone else's normalcy? To what he'd lost?

"I wish Shauna was here," he said suddenly.

Alicia met his gaze. "Me, too. I'd like to meet her."

Damn. He'd just opened the door to dangerous ground. The last thing he needed was to introduce his supposedly no-strings-attached lover to his twelve-year-old daughter, even if Shauna would be happy that he'd found someone. Of course, his daughter didn't know how truly messed up her daddy was.

He responded in a roundabout way, "I just miss her, that's all. Having her here while I'm working wouldn't be in her best interest."

"No, of course not."

Alicia hugged *Casablanca* to her chest, and the isolation in her body language made him think of the airport scene where Bogart's character sent Bergman's character away.

"He didn't let her stay with him," he said.

She blinked. "What?"

He gestured to her T-shirt. "He told her she would regret not getting on the plane. Maybe not today or maybe not tomorrow, but soon and for the rest of her life."

"You know the dialogue?" She didn't uncross her arms. If anything, she hugged herself a little tighter.

"Not word for word."

"That was pretty exact, Griffin."

"It's a famous movie. 'Here's looking at you, kid,' and all that. It's filled with notable lines."

"Like, 'Kiss me. Kiss me as if it were the last time?'"

He took a step back. "I forgot about that one." But he remembered kissing Alicia on the private island as if it were *their* last kiss. "Sometimes those old movies are corny."

She frowned. "And sometimes they become classics and future generations recite quotes from them."

He tried to downplay the romantic trap he'd just gotten himself into. "I might recall what the characters said, but I don't remember their names."

"Rick and Ilsa."

"Oh, yeah." How easily they settled back into his brain. "Why are we talking about this?"

"You brought it up."

He laid the blame back on her. "You're wearing the T-shirt."

She uncrossed her arms and went tough, moving into his personal space, taking up the air he was breathing, making the tension tighter.

"Get a clue, Griffin. You were supposed to kiss me when I brought up the kissing line."

"You know damn well I'm not clueless."

"Then what's your problem, profiler?"

"Maybe I don't like being goaded."

"Into a kiss?"

"Into whatever." They both knew this wasn't about a movie-mimicked lip lock. This was about feeling like Rick and Ilsa. About letting each other go in the end. About starting something that was destined for a painful finish.

She just stared at him, and he cursed inside.

"Screw it." He cursed out loud, too. Then grabbed Alicia and kissed her.

She didn't rebuff him. She didn't shove him backward and tell him to piss off, which, in his mind, would've been well deserved. But apparently her hurt, her anger, her fear was as erotically charged as his, and she pressed against him as he seized her mouth.

The kiss wasn't enough. He pulled her T-shirt over her head, knowing their joining was going to be anything but tender, anything but calm, anything but loving.

She sported a simple black bra. To Griffin, it looked like wicked lingerie. He tugged on her drawstring shorts and exposed her panties. They looked wicked, too. He slid his hand inside and made her wet.

A profanity escaped her lips, and the frustrated encouragement, the naughty word, ignited his blood.

He removed her panties and lifted her onto the nightstand. Instinctively, she opened her legs nice and wide so he could get a condom out of the drawer, and he thought it was the most erotic thing she'd ever done.

He closed the drawer, shoved down his sweats, tore open the protection and slid between her thighs. She was still wearing her basic bra, and he still had on his FBI T-shirt, but down below, he was already deep inside her.

She wrapped her arms around him, and air swooshed out of her lungs. On the beat of breathless insanity, their mouths met. The taste was hot and thrilling, so he took more and more. So did she.

"I wish I didn't need this so badly," Alicia said.

"Me, too." Griffin focused on the pleasure of his body pounding into hers. "But it feels good."

"Really good," she agreed.

"Better than good." The nightstand rattled from the motion.

She sucked on the side of his neck. "Outrageously good. You should see what I'm doing to you."

"I don't need to see." He knew that by the time they were done, he would have marks on his skin. But he didn't give a damn if she branded him. He was too aroused to curb the sensation it caused. "I don't think I've had a hickey since high school."

"Then you're due." She sucked on the same tortured spot.

"Damn." He all but moaned.

"You're easy, McSafety."

"Easy?" He pushed his penis full hilt, full force, full everything. "What I am is *hard.* You make me insatiable."

"For now," she said, as if she were trying to convince herself that eventually the hunger would stop.

"Yes, for now," he agreed, as the sex got even hotter and they climaxed in blasting waves.

When it ended, he wanted more. Not right away. He needed to restart his engine. But soon enough, he was back in business with another condom and Alicia straddling his lap in bed. She wanted more, too.

"Good thing we have two," he said.

"Two what?"

"Beds." At this second stage, they were completely naked. Her bra and his T-shirt had been tossed by the wayside.

"Why do we usually do it in mine?"

"Because we usually sleep in yours. And who cares? We're in mine now."

Her breasts bounced up and down, her nipples grazing his chest. She was like his favorite ice cream dessert with mounds of whipped cream and fresh-picked cherries on top. He wanted to make her come so he could watch her melt all over him.

"Griffin?"

"Hmm?"

"Are you going to go back to being celibate after we're not together anymore?"

His heart did a quick, unmanly flop. "You shouldn't ask me something like that." Especially when she was riding him. But as he looked into her soulful brown eyes, he asked her the same question. "Are you?"

"You have to answer first."

"Probably for a while." A long, long while, he thought. "Replacing you is going to be tough."

"Same here."

He cupped her rear and nudged her farther onto his erection. "Maybe I'll hire a girl who looks like you to keep me satisfied."

"That isn't funny." But she laughed anyway, her gorgeous wild hair falling forward and framing her face. "Besides, it's illegal."

"Oh, you're right. What was I thinking?" He rolled over and took her with him without missing a coital beat. "Then maybe I'll get a blowup doll. At least she won't talk in the middle of it."

"She won't do anything in the *beginning, middle* or *end* of it." Alicia nipped his chin when he tried to kiss her. "And you'd probably pop her like a balloon."

He ignored her silly sarcasm and managed to get the kiss. And, oh, what a kiss. Rick and Ilsa would have been proud. Or mortified. Or both.

Now, some of those damnable quotes were spinning in his head, his subconscious latching on to them like a tape-recorded message. Word-for-word. Rick said, *"How long was it we had, honey?"* and Ilsa replied, *"I didn't count the days."* And then, Rick's revealing response. *"Well, I did. Every one of them..."*

Was Griffin counting the days? Yes, he thought. He was. And it hurt like hell.

"I don't want to talk anymore," he told Alicia.

"I didn't say anything."

No, of course. It was Rick and Ilsa who were yapping at him.

He stroked her cheek, as gently as he could. He couldn't bear to be frantic, not this time. "I just want to make love with you."

She shivered, as if he'd just touched a place in her heart where no one else had ever been. "I'm not stopping you."

"I know." But he wished that she wanted him to stop. That he wanted to stop himself. But he couldn't.

Not even with the reminder that their days were numbered.

Chapter 10

When Alicia wasn't agonizing over falling irreversibly in love with Griffin, she was stressing about the possibility of receiving another correspondence from the killer—or whoever he was.

"I'm not handling this very well," she told Nalani as they headed up the stairs to Alicia's room. They'd spent the afternoon at the resort's yacht club. But not for fun. For Alicia's job. Still, it should have at least seemed like fun.

"The waiting is getting to you?"

Alicia nodded. It had been only two days since she'd gotten the original letter, but it was starting to seem like forever. "It's just this feeling, you know? That there's a madman thinking about me." She hesitated. "Or watching me."

"I didn't see anyone watching you," Nalani assured her.

But that didn't mean he wasn't around, Alicia thought. "I don't know what's worse. Not knowing if he's the Sex on the Beach Killer or wondering who else he might be."

Nalani escorted her into her room, and they closed the door. "You'll feel better when Agent Malone gets here and you can be alone with him."

But that didn't happen.

Once Griffin returned from his workday, Alicia barely gave him time to settle in. She instantly quizzed him about the investigation.

"Did the lab find anything on the letter?" she asked. "Fingerprints? DNA?"

"Nothing conclusive."

"What about the man from the disco? Is there any news on him?"

Griffin responded like the agent/lover that he was. "No, but the police are doing what they can to find out who he is." He reached out to move a stray hair away from her eyes. "You need to quit thinking about this, Alicia."

"I know. But I can't seem to focus on much else." Except for the fear of falling in love, and that wasn't helping, either.

"How about a diversion?"

"Like what?"

"We could build a sand castle."

She blinked, surprised by his suggestion. "Last time we argued when we tried to do that."

"We won't argue this time. I promise."

Hesitant, she glanced toward the window. "It's getting late."

"Are you afraid of being on the beach at night?"

Was she? She glanced back at him. "Maybe a little, but I know I shouldn't be." People weren't getting killed for making sand castles. The beach was safe for normal activity.

"We've got plenty of daylight left, and once the sun goes down, we can light the castle with candles. We can make the beach feel safer for you at night. Brighter, prettier. They should have some candles at the gift shop."

Alicia relaxed. He'd just created a fairy-tale image, clearing a path in her frazzled mind. "Are we going to get those little kiddie pails, too?"

"Why not? They'll work as forms." He walked over to the minibar and picked up the ice bucket. "This might come in handy. Oh, and we can ask the hotel for some kitchen utensils to use as sculpting tools. I'm sure I can wrangle a shovel out of them, too."

She laughed. "Why not get a bulldozer while you're at it? We could make a *really* big castle if we had one of those."

"Hey," he scolded, teasing her back. "This is serious stuff."

She smiled. "Then let's do it."

After buying and borrowing everything they needed, they headed to the beach with the supplies.

Griffin chose what he claimed was the perfect location. "If we're too far away from the shore, we'll have to dig too deep to hit the water table," he said. "And if we're too close, we could get wiped out by the tide."

"I remember that you picked a spot like this on the private island, too."

"Yes, but this time, we're going to have a castle to show for it."

Once the hole was dug, he taught her how to "hand stack"—to scoop wet sand out of the hole to create a foundation.

He knelt beside her. "You need to pull it toward you and move really fast so you don't lose the water."

"There goes my manicure," she joked as sand squished between her fingers. She glanced up and smiled. Playing on the beach with Griffin was much-needed therapy.

"That's good," he told her. "You're getting the hang of it."

"Thanks." He, of course, had the method down pat. She watched him with fascination. "How did you learn to do this?"

"When Shauna and I first moved to the beachfront property where we live now, there was a sand-sculpting contest going on, and we were blown away by the entries. Not just castles, but all sorts of things. Shauna said, 'Daddy, I want to learn to do that,' so we attended a workshop and learned the basics."

Alicia took a chance and asked him about his wife. "Did you move to the beach soon after Katie died?"

He nodded, answering her upfront. But he'd promised that they wouldn't argue. "Shauna and I couldn't stay at the other house. Neither of us could take living there anymore. Especially me. Every time I walked in the door, it was like reliving the moment I…"

He didn't finish his explanation, but she understood what he meant. Every time he walked into his old house, he was finding Katie's body all over again.

"I'm sorry, Griffin. Truly sorry for what happened to your wife."

He didn't blame her for using the "sorry" word he hated so much. He said, "Thank you," instead. "I know you really mean that. It's just not something you're saying to be polite."

"I do mean it."

In the background, the beach got quieter, except for the waves. The ocean swayed in its usual rhythm.

Alicia stopped scooping sand from the hole. But she didn't halt the conversation. She needed to know more about Griffin's wife, more about the woman who haunted his eyes. "How did you meet Katie?"

He quit scooping, too. "She was a police secretary when I was a cop. She was part of my life for so long, almost everything I do or did seems connected to her." He glanced at the mound in front of them. "Except for this. Making sand castles belongs to Shauna and me."

Alicia couldn't help her next words. "And now it's something you and I will always have, too."

He met her gaze, and they stared at each other. In the interim, the moment turned awkward.

She tried to repair the emotional damage. "I didn't mean that the way it sounded."

"No, you're right. It is something we'll always have. Something we'll always remember." He took an audible breath. "A castle in Fiji." He glanced at the mound of sand again. "If we ever get it built."

Alicia longed to touch him. But she didn't because her hands were gummy. Or maybe because her heart was warning her not to get too close, not to use this as an excuse to fall completely in love with him.

"Just show me how to finish making it," she said.

He explained how to build towers of various sizes, and

they went to work, using their hands, an array of molds and carving tools.

Next, he taught her how to construct a wall, and she helped him layer the sand-made bricks. He even carved archways and dug a moat. As time went by, their creation got more and more beautiful.

Alicia glanced up and noticed the sun was starting to set. Soon the darkening horizon would meet the ocean. A light breeze blew, making the salty scent more pronounced in the air.

There weren't many people on the beach at this hour, but those who were around stopped by to watch, to ask questions or to compliment them on their castle.

As the last of the spectators drifted away, Alicia decorated the towers with seashells.

Griffin retrieved the votive candles they'd purchased from the gift shop. He placed them inside the archways, protecting them from the wind.

After lighting the wicks, he and Alicia got up and stepped back. He glanced over at her, and she looked at him, a connection neither of them could seem to break.

As the flames flickered, as the castle they'd created shimmered in the oncoming night, she quit fighting what was in her heart. In that bittersweet moment, she knew that she loved him.

The following day, Alicia and Griffin spent a few hours with Nalani and her family. They lived in a river town, and their home offered a picturesque view of the water and a spacious backyard.

Nalani's husband went by his Christian name, Joseph, and readily answered to Joe. He was the same height as

Nalani, with short dark hair, friendly brown eyes and an equally welcoming nature. They seemed well suited to each other and comfortably in love. Alicia both admired and envied them.

Their kids, six-year-old Timmy and four-year-old Teresa, grinned and giggled and thoroughly enjoyed themselves. In Fiji, children were treated with warmth and care. It wasn't uncommon for babies to land in the tender arms of strangers.

Nalani prepared a picnic-style meal, and everyone gathered at an outdoor table.

Teresa climbed up onto Griffin's lap, and he held her while he ate. She bumped him a few times during her incessant wiggling and knocked some food from his fork, but he didn't seem to mind. He handled the child, the meal and the conversation just fine. In fact, he looked like he was in his element.

Alicia's heart surged into marriage mode, and Nalani caught her gaze from across the table. Then the lady officer turned to Griffin and said, "Inspector Inoke told me that you have a daughter."

"I do. Shauna. She's twelve." He rested his chin on the top of Teresa's head. "But I remember when she was this age." The little girl took a mango slice from his plate and ate it. "We always wanted a boy, too." He glanced at Timmy, who was chomping on a chicken-salad sandwich. "But after our daughter was born, my wife wasn't able to bear more children."

Alicia wondered why Katie couldn't have more kids, but she wasn't going to ask about it now. Later, she would question him. At least to a small degree, Griffin was willing to talk about Katie.

"There's always time for you to have a son," Nalani said. "All you need is a new wife."

Alicia wanted to kick the other woman under the table, but Joe more or less did it for her.

"Listen to you," he said to Nalani. "Trying to tie him down. Maybe the special agent doesn't want to get married again."

"I was just saying that if he wanted a son…"

"No more wives in my future," Griffin commented politely.

"For me, too." Joe made a typically male joke. "I have my hands full with the one I have."

Nalani jabbed her husband, and everyone laughed, including Alicia. What else could she do but behave as if she wasn't affected?

The subject changed, but it stayed on Alicia's mind. No more wives in Griffin's future. No more commitment. Being in love with him would go nowhere.

When the visit with Nalani's family ended, Griffin and Alicia headed back to the hotel. She glanced out of the car window and watched the river go by.

"They're nice people," he said.

She turned to look at him. "Yes, they are."

He didn't mention Nalani's obvious setup and, of course, neither did she. They both ignored it. But rather than suffer through uncomfortable silence, she broached the baby question. "Why couldn't your wife have more children?"

"Female troubles," he answered, without going into medical detail. "She had a hysterectomy about six months after Shauna was born."

"I never got pregnant because Jimmy's sperm count

was low. We tried artificial insemination, but that didn't work, and he didn't want to discuss other options. No donor sperm, no adoption." When the maternal ache that used to plague her came back, she tried to will it away. "It was tough for me at first. But I'm over it now."

"Yeah, me, too. There's no reason for me to be a dad again." He frowned at the road. "You know, since I'm not getting married again."

Apparently he'd decided not to ignore the marriage talk completely.

"Of course, Shauna would probably love having a little brother or sister," he added. "Sometimes she gets lonely being an only child. But I can't do anything about that."

Yes, he could, she thought. But she kept her mouth shut. She understood how his daughter felt, being an only child herself. And it made her want to meet Shauna even more.

Griffin's cell phone rang, interrupting their conversation. It was just as well, she supposed. Things were getting uncomfortable again.

He answered, "Agent Malone."

Alicia couldn't hear the other party, but she could tell by his expression that it was a serious call.

Extremely serious.

"Hold tight. I'm about ten minutes away." Pause. "I've got Ms. Greco with me." Another pause. "Yes, meet us in the security office. I'll be there as soon as I can."

He hung up and said, "That was Robert Lomu."

Her pulse jumped. "The hotel manager?"

He nodded, then reached over and put his hand on her knee. "A letter just arrived for you in the mail. Robert said the envelope looks the same as before. Typewritten with no return address."

The killer, she thought. Or the pretend killer.

Griffin took his hand away and called Inspector Inoke, then drove to their destination, with Alicia chock full of anxiety beside him.

When they arrived, he removed gloves and an evidence bag from his car and escorted her to where Robert and the chief of hotel security were waiting.

Griffin collected the letter, but he didn't open it. Instead, he drove Alicia to the police station with him, and she was left alone in an unoccupied office while he and Inspector Inoke did their law enforcement thing.

Griffin, of course, told her to relax, to "hold tight," until he came back.

"You have to let me know what it says," she responded.

"I will," he promised. He even lifted her chin and gave it a gentle tap, coaxing a brave smile out of her.

But after he was gone, the comfort of his touch vanished. She tried not to fidget, but it was a lost cause. She sat in a straight-back chair on the other side of an empty desk, jiggling her foot and wondering how long it would take until the contents of the letter were revealed to her.

The anticipation was killing her.

No, Alicia thought. *Don't use "killing," not even in your mind.* It was bad enough that the offender was called the Sex on the Beach Killer.

To keep herself occupied, she glanced out the window, which offered a view of the parking lot and patrol cars coming and going.

But that only distracted her for a few seconds. She

reached for a magazine that had been provided for her and paged through it, trying to read various articles. But her mind kept drifting.

The wait went on forever, or so it seemed.

Finally Griffin entered the room, and she got out of her seat. He had one of those indiscernible expressions on his face, but at least he'd kept his promise.

He handed her a piece of paper, and she took it, realizing it was some sort of police report. A transcript of the letter was typed at the bottom.

"So this is it," she said, stating the obvious, and began to read.

Dear Ms. Greco,
Have you been waiting to hear from me? What about Agent Malone? Has he been a diligent profiler, becoming me in his mind?

Alicia glanced up at Griffin, and he met her gaze. Before she caught a ghostly flash in the blue, she broke eye contact and returned to the words on the page, compelled to keep going.

I've been researching his job, and I have to say that with each passing day, I find profiling more and more intriguing. Behavioral science seems like a human chess game, with men like Malone trying to predict men like me.
What will be my next move?

Alicia blew out the breath in her lungs. She didn't want to think about his next move.

Last time, I said that I would tell you a bit about myself. When I was a boy, I lived in what most people would call a good neighborhood. But not everyone in our neighborhood was good. A woman who lived down the street from us seduced my father with her fancy red car and sleazy clothes. Sometimes her blouses were so tight, her buttons would strain or pop right off. Then she would pretend it was an accident. That she hadn't meant to expose a portion of her breasts.

How slutty is that? I wanted to shove those buttons down her throat and make her choke on them.

When Mother found a naked picture of her that Father had hidden in our garage, Mother slashed it to bits. I remember how she ran to the kitchen to get a knife from a cutlery set she kept on the counter. I stood back and watched the whore's picture die.

The image made Alicia cringe, but once again she kept reading.

Father continued the affair, and later there were more women, more sluts. I hated those whores, almost as much as I hated Father.

After he walked out on us, Mother tried to cleanse the world of filth. Sometimes she brought pornography home and burned it in the fireplace. Other times she hacked it up. She never let me touch any of it because she said it might arouse my private parts. She reminded me over and over again that I was a boy and men and boys were weak.

But I am not weak. I have learned to be strong.

Would Mother be proud of me for punishing people who have sex in public? I don't know, and I don't care. I'm not a mama's boy, and don't let Agent Malone tell you that I am. I'm doing this for me, not for Mother.

Goodbye, Ms. Greco. It's been nice spending this fleeting time with you. You'll be leaving soon, won't you? Returning to your old life?

But surely Agent Malone will be staying in Fiji for a while. I hope so. Because I want him to be around for what happens next. It's just too bad you won't be here to find the bodies.

The correspondence ended with *Yours truly,* leaving Alicia with goose bumps along her arms and a shiver in her heart.

Chapter 11

"Can you tell if the killer wrote this?" Alicia asked. "Or is this letter just as unclear as the last one?"

"It's him," Griffin responded, and watched her chest heave with a quick, shaky breath. He wanted to take her in his arms and hold her tight against him, but he knew that she needed answers first. Hugging her wouldn't be enough.

"He said something that identifies him? That only the killer would say?"

"Yes, but I can't tell you what portion of the letter that was. I can't explain it to you." But as soon as Griffin had read about the buttons popping off of the woman's too-tight tops and how the man/boy in the communiqué wanted to make her choke on them, he knew it was the offender. The Sex on the Beach Killer collected buttons from his female victims. He rummaged through their clothes after they were dead, and if their garments contained buttons, he removed one. If the women's clothes didn't have buttons, he took a small patch of material as a substitute. In those instances, Griffin suspected that he glued the fabric onto a generic button, creating what he needed. Souvenirs, little treasures to keep locked away somewhere, and now Griffin understood the psychological significance associated with them.

"The killer doesn't seem to care that I'm leaving Fiji," she said, pulling him back to their conversation.

"That's because he doesn't plan on sending you another letter." Griffin wasn't alarmed that the offender had commented on when Alicia was going home. She'd mentioned how long she would be in Fiji in the TV interview she'd given after she'd found the bodies. "You were a pawn in the chess game he referred to, but now he wants to play a direct game with me."

"All that stuff he said about his childhood. It's like Norman Bates in *Psycho*. The mother thing."

"Norman Bates's character was inspired by serial killer Ed Gein. But so was Leatherface in *The Texas Chainsaw Massacre* and Buffalo Bill in *Silence of the Lambs*."

"Wow." Alicia made a crack. "Ed Gein must have been a lovely man."

Griffin shook his head, and they both sputtered into postanxiety laughter. God, he would miss her when she went home. But their affair wasn't meant to go beyond this point.

She went serious. "Do you think he knows that we're lovers?"

"No. He's interested in us because of the investigation, not because he considers us a couple." Which told Griffin that if the offender had seen Alicia and Griffin together, he'd assumed that Alicia was under Griffin's protection, which, of course, she was. It also told him that the offender wasn't acquainted with anyone at the hotel who suspected that the profiler and the witness were sexually involved.

"Is he originally from the States? I just automatically assumed that he was, but I never asked you before."

"He behaves like an American serial killer, so yes, I think he's from the States. It's also possible that he's British or Australian, but that he has a strong taste for America. But no matter where's he's from, he lives in the Pacific now. Probably in Fiji."

"Does he have a job?"

"Most likely he's in a field that brought him to the Pacific. Import/export. Or maybe tourism."

"That covers a lot of ground."

"Yes, it does."

"So what happens now?" she asked. "To me, I mean."

"Nothing. You're still a witness who's being provided with protection while you're here. When you're not with me, you'll be with Officer Molias. Nalani," he amended.

"Then I'll leave for Chicago and be far away from the killer?"

"Yes."

"I'll be far away from you, too."

He couldn't help himself. He finally reached out to hug her. "Eventually I'll be going home, too. No matter how you look at it, we'll be living separate lives. Fiji will be over for both of us."

* * *

Around 11:00 p.m., Griffin got ready for bed in his bathroom while Alicia soaked in the tub in hers. It had been a long, exhausting day for both of them.

After he finished brushing his teeth, he entered her room through the adjoining door. When he noticed a familiar box of candles on the dresser/TV stand, he picked it up. The glass-cupped candles were vanilla-scented votives, left over from the sand castle experience.

No point in letting them go to waste, he thought. So he scattered them about the room and lit each one.

Soon Alicia emerged wearing a short yellow night-gown decorated with bits of feminine lace. Her hair was still pinned up from the bath, a few stray tendrils damp at the ends.

"It smells good in here," she said.

"Because of the candles we bought."

"I know. I see them." She gave him a girl-soft smile. "It will be even nicer when we turn out the lights."

He darkened the room, and they got into bed.

She lifted the covers a smidgen. "Who knew FBI agents could be so romantic?"

"And who knew witnesses could be so pretty?" He removed the clip she'd left in her hair, allowing her long, dark tresses to fall around her shoulders.

"I'll bet there have been other pretty witnesses."

"Not that I ever noticed." But he'd been married for most of his career, and after Katie had been murdered, he'd shut himself off. Yet here he was, engaged in an affair with Alicia.

"Do you have any secrets, Griffin?"

"What?" he responded, caught off guard by her question.

"You know, things you've never told another living soul."

He'd never admitted that he felt responsible for Katie's death. He'd never revealed to anyone that she'd asked him to stay home the weekend she'd died.

"No," he lied. "Why? Do you?"

"Me? I'm too much of a blabbermouth. I'm not good at keeping things in."

Griffin realized he was still holding her hair clip, clutching the metal ornament between his fingers. He set it on the nightstand nearest to him.

"Sometimes you're good at keeping things in," he said.

"I am?"

He nodded. Like now, he thought. She hadn't told him her biggest secret. She hadn't professed that she was falling in love with him. But she was. Suddenly he could see it in her eyes. He could hear it in her voice. But that didn't mean he was the right man for her.

Far from it, he thought.

Griffin wasn't emotionally capable of giving Alicia what she needed. The man he used to be wanted to return her love. But the man he'd become since Katie had died couldn't bring himself to let it happen.

"Are you coming with me tomorrow?" she asked, changing topics. "Or will Nalani be there instead?"

She was referring to the beach-party barbecue the resort hosted on a bimonthly basis, an event Alicia was including in her final rating. "We'll both be there. Inoke is going to have some other officers in place, too."

"Why? Do you think the killer is going to show up?"

"Truthfully, I doubt he'll make an appearance. But we'll be keeping our eye out for anyone who could be him. Just in case."

"What about the man from the disco? He's still a possible suspect, isn't he?"

"Yes. We'll be looking for him, too."

"It's weird that I met you because of a killer. I never thought something like that would ever happen to me."

"It's weird for me, too." Even though killers were part of his world, his dark realm. But they'd had this conversation before, so they went silent.

As candlelight danced softy on the walls, creating nighttime shadows, she spoke first. "I wonder what we'll both be doing years from now."

"How many years?"

"I don't know." She paused then said, "Five," as if she'd just grabbed it out of the air. "Five years."

That seemed like a lifetime away, he thought. "Let's see. I'll still be an agent, and you'll be…"

"What?" she asked, watching him closely.

"A wife and mother," he said, meaning it. "You'll have everything you used to want. Only this time, you'll find the right guy, and it will work out for you."

Her eyes met his, and emotion crackled between them.

He thought about the way Nalani had tried to play marriage matchmaker. She, too, was aware that Alicia was destined to be a wife.

The bride in question protested. "That's not what I want."

"Yes, it is." He knew that she would marry him if that

were what he was offering. But he was predicting that she would spend her life with someone else.

"I'll prove you wrong." She pulled at the sheet, almost tugging his portion of the bedding away from him. "I'll stay single and independent."

"I didn't mean to upset you. I'm just saying what's what. If I look you up in five years, you'll be a kitchen-cozy wife and mom. You'll be what you were meant to be."

"If that's how my future plays out, then why would I need to hear from you?"

"You wouldn't." But even as he said it, his heart tensed. "And you won't. I was being hypothetical about looking you up."

"Was Katie a kitchen-cozy wife and mom?" she asked.

His heart tensed even more. "Yes. She was completely devoted to our marriage and to our daughter. That was who she was."

"So I'm like her?"

He nodded. "Yeah, I guess you are." Only Alicia's future husband wasn't going to leave her at home one weekend to die. "But you're going to have a long, happy life."

"You can't know that, Griffin."

"I can think it. I can believe it." He studied her in the flickering light. By now, the room was steeped in vanilla, heavy with melting wax. "I can hope it comes true for you."

"And what am I supposed to hope comes true for you?"

"You can wish good things for my daughter."

"Yes, but what about *you*," she persisted.

"Nothing," he responded, dismissing his dreams. "I don't need you to wish for anything for me."

He couldn't regain the part of himself he'd lost, not even for Alicia.

In the morning while Griffin was in the shower, Alicia sat on her veranda, talking to Zoë.

"I think he figured out that I love him," she said into the phone.

"Wait, hold on," her friend responded. "You *love* him? Since when? The last time we talked, you were denying it."

"That was then. This is now."

"What makes you think he figured it out?"

"From the things he said last night." About her being happily married to someone else in the future. "He doesn't want to be with me after this. When I leave Fiji, it'll be over. Totally over."

"Oh, honey, I'm so sorry. Is there anything I can do?"

"No. I just needed a shoulder to cry on." Only she wasn't crying. She wouldn't dare, not at the risk of Griffin coming onto the veranda and catching her blubbering into the phone. No, she would save her tears for Chicago. "It hurts so bad."

"I know. Believe me, I do. If Breeze and I hadn't—" Zoë stalled. "Maybe Griffin is going through what you went through at first. Maybe he loves you, too, but he won't admit it."

"I don't think he's the denial type." How could a man with an advanced degree in behavioral science not know his own heart?

"Maybe he needs a little more time." Obviously Zoë was trying to make her feel better.

"I'll be gone in two days." She glanced out at the view, where the Fijian sun had risen in a ball of orange fury. "There isn't much time left."

"A lot can happen in two days. Honestly it can."

Alicia managed a weak smile. "Thanks, Zoë. But I better go. I need to get dressed for the day."

They said goodbye and hung up, and she went back inside.

Her timing was perfect. Or maybe it was out of sync. Griffin entered her room through his, wearing shorts, sandals and a loose-fitting Hawaiian shirt.

"You don't look like a G-man today," she said, even though she suspected that he was armed beneath the *Magnum P.I.* print.

"I'm not supposed to. We're going to a beach barbecue. But first I'm going to hang out here and get some work done. On my laptop."

"You've got a killer to analyze, then reanalyze."

"Exactly. You're getting to know my job pretty well."

"It comes with the territory. You and your job go hand in hand." She wanted to touch him so badly she ached in the pit of her rejected soul.

He came forward and drew her into his arms instead, tugging her body close to his. She was still wearing her baby-doll nightgown, and he ran his hands along the silky fabric, cupping her rear in the process.

A reminder that their relationship was supposed to be about sex.

She wished that she'd never fallen in love with him. Sleeping with him should've been enough. He gave her a hunky kiss, and she shivered from the impact. Especially when she felt the masculine rat-a-tat-tat of his heartbeat.

He released her and stepped back. "Should we order a light breakfast?" he asked, frowning a little. "Something to hold us over until the barbecue? Oatmeal and orange juice?"

"That sounds fine. Healthy." Was he frowning because of the effect she had on him? Did it worry him that she made his heart machine-gun his chest? God, she hoped so.

He walked away to call room service, and she struggled to hold on to Zoë's words, to her positive *A lot can happen in two days,* comment.

Could it? Would it?

Alicia went into her bathroom to wash up and do her makeup and hair. By the time she was fully clothed and sparkling fresh, the food had been delivered to Griffin's room.

He was sitting at the table, buried in his work with his oatmeal half-eaten. He glanced up from his laptop.

"Wow," he said, scanning the golden length of her. "You look hot. Like a mermaid."

"Thanks." Was it possible to keep a man by wearing a bikini top and a sexy sarong tied around her waist? She didn't know, but she was giving it her best shot. She'd even gone a little wilder with her hair, making sure it was extra full and flirty.

"Your skin is shimmering."

"It's a sparkler lotion. It's supposed to enhance a tan. There's glitter in it."

When the same frown as before appeared on his face,

she smiled and sat down, lifting the lid off of her hot cereal. She added milk and sugar, stirred up it up real good and made a yummy sound when she spooned it into her mouth.

He returned to his work, but she saw him stealing glances at her from across the table.

Score one for the glitter, she thought.

After breakfast, she left him alone and went back to her own room to pass the time with TV.

Hours later, he surfaced from his laptop, but apparently he still had her on his mind.

"I want you totally naked tonight," he said. "With your hair fixed the way it is and even more of that shiny stuff on your skin."

She arched her eyebrows. "It'll get all over you."

"So I'll wash it off afterward. Just say yes and give me something to look forward to. Something to think about while we're at the barbecue."

She grinned. "Something sinful?"

"Yes, ma'am." He flashed an equally wicked grin.

"Then it's a date." Whatever she could do to leave a lasting impression, she thought, to turn two more days into a lifetime. To make him long for an affair that would last forever.

The crowd was an eclectic mix of adults, teenagers and children. The law enforcement in attendance blended into the environment. There were no uniformed cops.

Alicia had arrived with Griffin, but they separated for a while, and Alicia spent some time with Nalani.

They stood near the ocean, talking, while surf tunes blazed on a sound system and kids gathered for prearranged games. The aroma of charbroiled food hung in the air. Soon the buffet table would be filled with a feast.

"You're not angry at me, are you?" Nalani asked.

Alicia studied the other woman's concerned expression. "No. Why would I be?"

"For what I said to Agent Malone about getting married again."

"You were just trying to help. There's no reason for me to be angry. I've been sad about Griffin's reaction, though."

"I can understand why. But maybe he'll change his mind."

"My friend Zoë said that, too. I talked to her this morning about it."

"Then you should try to stay positive. Being sad won't help."

"I'm doing the best I can under the circumstances." She was hoping to turn sex into everlasting love.

Reflective, both women gazed quietly at the sea. As always, it was breathtaking. Waves broke along rocks that bordered the cliffs.

"Have you ever wondered what it would be like to be a mermaid?" Alicia asked. "Griffin said I looked like a mermaid today."

"I'm sure he meant a pretty one."

"Is there any other kind?"

"There's the kind they call a Fiji of *F-E-E-J-E-E* mermaid." Nalani spelled out the second Feejee. "They're grotesque creatures that used to be featured at sideshows."

"Really?" Now being a lady with a tail didn't sound so appealing. "Are they part of your culture?"

"No. The first Fiji mermaid was a hoax. It was exhibited by P. T. Barnum."

"The circus guy?"

Nalani nodded. "He came up with the name, and it stuck. Now it's a generic term for those types of fake mermaids."

"What did the first one look like?"

Nalani tightened her body, made spastic motions with her hands and twisted her features, creating a horrible face. "Like this."

Alicia laughed. "That bad, huh?"

Nalani laughed, too. "No one is sure how it was made. It might have been constructed from papier-mâché and fish parts. Or it might have been the head of a monkey and the torso of a baby orangutan with a fish tail sewn on."

"That's gross."

"It's better to be the kind of mermaid Agent Malone called you."

"No kidding." Alicia turned away from the picture-perfect ocean and saw Griffin heading their way. "Speak of the devil."

"I'll make myself scarce," Nalani said. "I can tell he's coming to see you."

"Okay. I'll talk to you later."

The female officer walked away, leaving Alicia and her lover alone.

Griffin got closer and said, "I figured this was a good song to use to get your attention."

Alicia hadn't been tuned into the music. She stopped to listen. It was a guitar-riff instrumental. "Why? Is it supposed to mean something to me?"

"It's called 'FBI'. It was recorded by a sixties group called the Shadows. They had a few other hits, too."

Grotesque mermaids and a G-man surf song. How much stranger could things get?

"Agent Moondoggie," she teased. "I was wrong about you not looking like an FBI guy today."

"Agent *Mc*Moondoggie," he corrected, and smiled.

She smiled, too, and itched to run her fingers through his graying temples. But she kept her hands to herself.

"It's almost time to eat," he said. "They're filling the buffet now. Do you want to have lunch together?"

"Yes, of course." She wouldn't turn down an opportunity to be with him. She glanced over to where the line was already forming.

"Any luck with the crowd?" she asked. "Any suspicious characters?"

"Not so far. No one is behaving the way the offender would behave if he were here."

"And how *would* he behave?"

"He'd be milling around by himself, watching the activities. To most people, he wouldn't seem out of place, but he wouldn't be socializing, either. He'd be keeping a low profile."

"But you said that you didn't think he was going to show up, so I guess he won't be having lunch with us."

"No. I don't suspect that he will." Griffin gestured to the line, which had gotten bigger. The buffet was open now. "Ready?"

They joined the rest of the partygoers, purchased their meal tickets and got in line. The barbecue featured char-grilled beef, chicken and fish with crisp salads, pastas, curries and vegetables.

It took a while to reach the food, but when they did, Alicia filled her plate, intent on enjoying herself.

But as she turned toward the dessert table, she nearly dropped her meal. In the near distance was a man cutting across the beach and coming toward the barbecue. He was laughing and talking with a group of people who appeared to be his friends. He wasn't behaving the way Griffin claimed the killer would behave, but he was ominously familiar.

He was the man from the disco.

Chapter 12

"Are you sure he isn't the killer?" Alicia asked Griffin for at least the twentieth time.

"Yes, we're sure."

She sipped from a glass of water and told herself to relax. They were at the police station, where the man from the disco had been interviewed.

"How can you know for sure?"

"He has air-tight alibis for all of the murders. He wasn't even in the Pacific when the first four couples were killed."

"What about the night Paxton and Veronica were stabbed?"

"He was with friends. When you saw him, he'd just stepped outside to have a cigarette and was returning to the disco. His friends were at a booth on the other side of the club, and from there, they left and went out for a late dinner in Suva. His story checks out."

Alicia glanced out the window. Nighttime had fallen. They'd been at the station all day and part of the evening. "He doesn't fit the profile, either, does he?"

"No. Not at all. He's just another witness who was at the disco that night."

"Does he recall anyone who fits the profile?"

Griffin shook his head. "He watched Veronica so closely because he thought he recognized her from a bathing suit calendar a buddy of his had given him last Christmas."

"Was it her in the calendar?"

"Yes, it was."

Alicia had another question. "Why didn't he come forward? Didn't he know the police were looking for him?"

"No. He didn't. He and his friends went to a surf camp on a private island on the morning after the murders. They just got back today."

"So that's it. I remembered the wrong man under hypnosis, and the real killer is still out there."

"This isn't your fault. You can't be expected to remember everyone who was at the disco, especially a guy who was doing his damnedest not to be remembered."

"But I was supposed to be your best lead. Your best witness."

"You did what you could. And don't forget that the offender wrote to you. He gave us information about himself in those letters. He's going to get caught, Alicia. It's just a matter of time."

"How could I forget those letters?" She laughed, but the sound was humorless.

"Come on. Let's get out of here. Let's go back to the hotel. We can order some fancy food and cozy up with a bottle of wine."

"That works for me." She wasn't about to deny him. Or herself. She needed Griffin Malone; she needed her G-man. "I'm supposed to wear more glitter for you tonight."

"Yes, ma'am. You are." He leaned in to kiss her, and she tasted the heat of who he was, the passion of his flavor mingling with hers.

An hour later they settled into their rooms with an array of romantic appetizers, including a fruit and cheese platter accompanied by a medium-bodied Cabernet Sauvignon.

"This is nice," he said.

"It is. Very nice." A feeling she longed to capture for the rest of their lives. Alicia would move to Virginia with Griffin in a heartbeat. She would help him raise his daughter. She would bear him another child. She would be the wife and mother he claimed she was meant to be. But she only wanted it with him. She couldn't see herself with anyone else.

They finished eating and he asked, "Will you put the glittery stuff on now? But I want to watch, okay? So bring it out here."

Eager to please him, Alicia went into her bathroom to get the lotion. She fluffed her hair and refreshed her makeup, too.

When she returned, he was seated on the edge of her bed, looking like a hungry male in his prime.

"Strip for me," he said. "All the way naked."

Still dressed in her swimsuit and sarong, she indulged his fantasy, beginning with the string ties on her bikini top. After her breasts were bare, she removed the sarong and reached for her bikini bottoms.

Griffin watched every move she made, but Alicia didn't feel self-conscious. She felt good. Warm. Sexy. She wanted to be naked for him.

As she peeled off her bikini bottoms, he smiled. She wanted to climb in his lap, but she'd promised to use the lotion, so she uncapped the bottle.

She smoothed the substance all over, making her skin shimmer, turning herself into the pretty mermaid he desired.

"I want to remember you just like this," he said. "Forever in my mind."

Forever in your heart, she wanted to say, praying that he would fall in love with her before the night was through. Wishful thinking? Girlish dreams? She couldn't stop her hopeful seduction if she tried.

She walked over to him and unbuttoned his shirt, tossing the Hawaiian-print garment aside. He'd already removed his firearm earlier, so he wasn't wearing his Glock. But his cock, she thought, sliding her hand along the waistband of his shorts. Now that was another matter.

She got on her knees in front of him, and his stomach muscles rippled with a sudden intake of breath.

"Damn," he said, the word catching in his throat.

Alicia licked his abs, and he shivered. Teasing him was fun. Pleasing him was going to be even better.

She removed his shorts and boxers in one skilled swoop and made his erection spring free. Empowered, she circled the tip with her tongue.

"You're making me crazy," he rasped.

"That's the idea." She took him all the way to the back of her throat, and he tunneled his hands in her hair.

She sucked him fast and deep, then sweet and slow,

then quick and hard again, using her hands to stimulate him even more. He kept losing his breath, and she knew he was fighting the urge to come.

"Stop," he said. "Oh, hell. You better stop."

She paused and looked up at him. "Are you sure you don't want me to keep going?" The other times she'd done this to him, he hadn't spilled into her. This time, she was willing to let him.

"Yes. No. Oh, damn, I don't know." His breathing went labored again. "Your mouth…"

"What about it?"

"You're getting lipstick all over me."

"You like that, don't you, Griffin?"

"Yes. It was one of my first fantasies about you."

"I know." She wet her mouth, making her lipstick glossier. "So let me do it some more."

"Okay," he said, falling under her spell. His eyes drifted half-closed, but he was still watching her.

Alicia lowered her head and performed the best oral sex she was capable of giving. He moved with her, consumed by the hot, pulsing rhythm.

"You're bewitching me," he said. "With your glittery skin, your long, pretty hair and your…"

Lipstick, she thought, as his body tensed, then jerked in an orgasmic spasm. The hands in her hair tightened, and the salty taste of him filled her mouth.

She swallowed his essence and nuzzled his stomach when it was over, giving him a moment to regain his composure.

His eyes opened all the way, and they gazed at each other. She was still on her knees, and he was still half-hard.

She climbed onto his lap and kissed him. He looped

his arms around her waist and pulled her closer, until they tumbled backward onto the bed.

"It's my turn to do things to you," he said, his blue eyes blazing with lust.

"Oh, yeah?"

"Yeah. Go get your lipstick."

"What?"

"You heard me."

"Why? What are you going to do with it?"

"Just get it and find out."

Curiosity got the better of her. "What color?"

"The pink stuff you were wearing will work just fine."

She arose and retrieved the item he requested, returned to bed and handed him the container.

"Twilight Temptation," she said.

He smiled. "That's the name of it? Seriously?"

"Yes. Seriously."

He removed the top, rolled the bottom of the tube and checked out the waxy substance. "Pretty. Very pretty. Now, I need to put it to good use."

Alicia waited, her heart fluttering. She had no idea what to expect.

"Lie down," he told her.

She did what he asked, stretching her naked body onto the quilt. He leaned forward and drew a heart around her navel with the lipstick.

A *heart*. Sweet heaven. She nearly melted into the bed. Next he put an arrow through the drawing. But not crossways. He did it downward, so the arrow was pointing to the V between her thighs.

"It's a map of where I'm going to kiss you," he said.

"Oh." Her voice went girlishly weak.

He colored around her nipples, making the areolas pinker. He also painted a little onto her mouth, studying her like Michelangelo on an erotic day.

He discarded the Twilight Temptation and pressed his long, hard body next to hers.

"I hardly know where to start." He kissed her lips— softly, romantically—then moved down and sucked on a pearled nipple.

Yes, Alicia thought. She wanted to marry this man. She wanted to honeymoon with him forever. Castles on the beach and now this. She couldn't think of a more enchanted moment. The glittery lotion on her skin left sparkles on him, too. It made him look like a knight from a mystical world, his blue eyes shining bright.

He lavished her other breast, then worked his way to her stomach, where he teased the center of the lipstick heart, dipping his tongue into her belly button.

She knew what came next, and she tingled in anticipation. He glanced up at her, and she held her breath, her pulse beating between her legs.

He lowered his head, and she released the air in her lungs. He licked her, making her wetter than she already was. The warmth of his mouth, the moisture of his tongue and the hunger in his touch sent shivers straight to her core. She climaxed instantly, but he kept going, giving her more and more pleasure.

He lifted her legs onto his shoulders, making the act even more sensual, more primitive. Alicia was sprawled out like a tattooed sacrifice. While he kissed her in the most intimate way, he traced the heart, running his fingers along her stomach, inciting another wave of shivers.

How could she not love him?

Alicia reached out to touch his hair, to comb through the thickness. He filled himself with her flavor, licking her most sensitive spot.

She jerked her hips and watched him through another orgasm, her mind blurring in prismatic colors. She knew there would never be another Griffin Malone. Not for her. He was it.

"Turn over," he said afterward.

"What?"

"I want to, you know…"

"Do me stallion style?" She glanced at his penis. He was aroused again, big and beautifully hard.

"I don't think that's a real position."

"It sounds sexier than doggy style."

"Not if the dogs are wolves."

"Are you a wolf, Griffin?"

"Turn over and find out."

She got on her hands and knees, and he removed a condom from the drawer. She could hear him tearing into the package.

When he got behind her and planted his hands on her hips, she took a steadying breath. Soon he would be inside her. She was already reeling from the oral pleasure he'd given her.

He entered her hard and deep, and she imagined how he looked, fitted against her, thrust full hilt.

"I wish I could see what you're doing to me," she said.

"I can see," he responded. "Do you want me to describe it to you?" He pushed deeper. "We look hot, Alicia. You and me. Joined together."

"Are you watching it going in and out?"

"Yeah, I'm watching." He gripped her hips a little tighter, giving himself plenty of leverage. "Damn, this turns me on."

The rocking motion was slick and carnal. He *was* a wolf, she thought. He was breathing her in, devouring her scent as he pumped hard and rough.

"Touch yourself," he said.

She gulped the air in her lungs.

"Do it," he commanded. "Make yourself come while I'm inside you."

Feeling shy yet sensual, embarrassed yet excited, Alicia reached down to put her hand there. Right there. On the same spot Griffin had stimulated earlier.

"That's right." He leaned forward and moved her hair away from the back of her neck so he could nip her skin. "That's perfect." He scraped his teeth along her spine. "Does it feel good? What you're doing to yourself?"

"Yes. But what you're doing to me feels incredible, too." Wild, she thought. Powerful. She wanted more and more.

And so did Griffin.

He decided to switch positions. He withdrew and turned her around so they could look into each other's eyes while she touched herself. Within seconds, he was inside of her again.

All the way in. All the way out.

They kissed, too, tongues tangling in perilous passion.

She wanted to tell him that she loved him, but she was afraid of saying it out loud, afraid that she would break down if he didn't repeat the sentiment.

Besides, he already knew that she loved him. Griffin, the profiler, knew everything there was to know about her.

He plunged deeper, caressing the inner walls of her sex, making it swell with honey-slick moisture.

She looked up at him, thinking how perfectly male he was. Muscles corded in his arms, and his abs tightened with each surging thrust. His face, those handsome features, exuded carnal concentration.

He climaxed, and she followed, lost in the hot, naked fury of Agent Malone.

Afterward, they separated. He got up to dispose of the protection, and she glanced down at her stomach and panicked.

The romantic image he'd drawn was smudged and faded, blurring into pink nothingness, making the heart he'd given her all but gone.

Griffin returned to bed and noticed the way Alicia was gazing at the smeared lipstick. He hadn't considered how a heart would affect her. But he should've.

"I'll buy you one to take home," he said.

"What?" She gave him a confused look.

"A heart."

"You can't buy someone a heart."

"Sure you can. I'll get you a piece of jewelry or something. We can go shopping tomorrow. We can spend the entire day together." Her last day in Fiji, he thought. He wanted to be with her as much as he could before she went back to Chicago and he never saw her again.

She didn't say anything, so he turned onto his side so he could face her. Needing to touch her, he skimmed her cheek with the back of his hand, running his knuckles along the softness of her skin.

"Let me buy you a heart," he said. If he couldn't give

her his own, at least he could give her one that was whole, that was shiny and bright. "Something to remember us by."

Her breath hitched. "Okay."

"We can shop during the day and go out in the evening. We'll find a classy club in Suva. We'll get dressed up and have a nice dinner. We can go dancing, too."

"Our first date," she said. "On our last night."

It was the best he could do. "This was never meant to go on forever. We have to accept it for what it is."

She nodded, but he could see that she was hanging on to hope. She wasn't letting go, not yet. She would stick it out to the very end and wait for him to change his mind.

He wanted to change his mind. God help him, he did. But he was scared, so damned scared of loving her.

She turned his world upside down. She made him long for a fresh start, for a clean break. But how could he make a life with her? Katie was still inside of him, burning a hole in his guilty heart.

"Can I buy you something, too?" she asked.

There was nothing she could purchase for him that would set him at ease, but he said, "If you want to."

She snuggled a little closer. "Has anyone ever given you a griffin?"

"Like a pendant or statue or something? Yes. I've got quite a few of them. Katie used to say that it was my spirit guide."

A griffin was a mythical creature with the head, beak, talons and wings of an eagle and the body of a lion. Male griffins had spikes on their backs instead of wings.

Mostly they were heroic symbols. In some cultures they depicted strength and courage. In others, they embodied wisdom. In Greek mythology they guarded nests of gold.

"Katie believed in griffins?" Alicia asked.

"She believed in all sorts of things. She used to talk about *Sint Holo*. He's a horned serpent in the Choctaw culture. He appears to wise young men." Griffin forced a casual laugh. "That pretty much leaves me out of the picture." He was no longer young nor was he particularly wise. Not these days.

"I can't do anything about *Sint Holo*," Alicia said. "But I can get you a griffin to add to your collection."

"I don't think you'll find one in Fiji."

"I think I will." She smiled. "I found you, didn't I?"

Yes, he thought. And look where that had gotten her— in love with the wrong man. But he kept telling himself that she would find the right man, that her future would be secure, that she would be happy.

Only when he envisioned her in someone else's arms, he anguished from the loss. Needing to touch her again, he kissed her. She kissed him back, and he captured her in a possessive embrace.

Alicia closed her eyes, and a short while later she fell asleep with her head on his shoulder. Griffin stayed awake purposely, trying to fool himself into believing that if he stretched the short time they had left, if he made the twilight hours count, it wouldn't hurt as badly in the end.

Alicia and Griffin shopped all day in Suva, going in and out of crowded retail shops on a busy street. A lot of vendors were aggressive, trying to sell them touristy junk, and others let them wander around by themselves.

Some of the jewelry prices were too good to be true, but that was because the gold was fake. Alicia allowed Griffin to take the lead. He seemed to know what was what. No way was an FBI agent going to be sucked into a scam.

While in one of the nicer stores, they looked at an array of heart jewelry: earrings, bracelets and pendants. But the vendor kept trying to steer them toward a dazzling pink sapphire and diamond ring in the shape of a heart and set in gold.

Griffin shook his head a few times, but as they continued to browse, he glanced back at the ring. So did Alicia.

The vendor showed them everything he had in the shape of a heart, but nothing impressed Griffin, nothing except the ring. Alicia saw him eyeing it again.

The vendor noticed, too. He took the ring out of the case again, being the salesman he was born to be. He was a middle-aged Indo-Fijian with a heavy accent and a genuine smile.

"It would look lovely on your lady," he said.

"Yes, it would." Griffin turned toward Alicia. "Do you want to try it on?"

Was he kidding? He knew darn well she did. She squeaked out a "Yes." The vendor handed it to her and she slipped it on her left hand, where her former wedding band used to be. It fit like Cinderella's slipper.

"Do you like it?" Griffin asked.

She managed another squeaky "Yes."

"Then I'll get it for you."

Alicia noticed that it was a costly piece. She couldn't help herself. She double-checked with Griffin.

"Are you sure?" she asked.

"I want you to have a keepsake."

"But it's expensive."

"I can afford it."

"I wasn't… I just…" She wanted him to realize how significant it seemed. But he was brushing it off as simple goodbye gift.

He seemed frustrated. "Do you want it or not?"

"Of course I do." She gazed at glittering stones and wished upon them like stars. "I want it very much."

"Then wear it. But with no strings attached." He snared her gaze. "Okay?"

She nodded, agreeing to the terms of his gift, even if she was praying that her wish would come true. That by tomorrow, the ring would represent a lifelong proposal.

"We still need to shop for you," she said.

"We won't find a griffin."

"A griffin?" the salesman chimed in. "I have a man's ring. Wait. Hold on. Let me get it." He walked away and came back with a thick gold band with the impression of the mythical beast on it. "It's an antique. An old signet ring."

"Oh, it's perfect," Alicia said. "Look at his eyes." They were blue, like Griffin's.

"They're blue topaz," the vendor told her, identifying the gems.

"That's my birthstone," Griffin said with a frown.

Alicia ignored his scowl. This ring was meant to be. "Try it on."

He put on it on his ring finger on his right hand, but it was a too tight. He couldn't get it past his knuckle.

She urged him on. "Try your left."

He hesitated. "It probably won't…"

"Try it." The vendor jumped in.

Griffin slipped it on, and it fit. But Alicia sensed that it would, just as her ring had fit her left hand without having to make any size adjustments.

He stared at the jeweled signet. "I haven't worn a ring since…" He turned to Alicia and said quietly, "I buried Katie with my wedding band because hers was stolen the day she was killed."

"Then wear this one as a replacement," she said. "From me. And from Katie." She spoke quietly, too. "I think she would approve."

"It's strange. To find this here, of all places." He lifted his gaze, and his eyes mirrored the griffin.

Alicia got chills. Katie was right. His namesake was his spirit guide.

She checked the price, grateful that it was within her budget. "Will you let me buy it for you?"

He nodded, and the purchase was made.

Afterward, Alicia and Griffin left the shop, their new gold rings shining in the sun.

Chapter 13

Griffin drove back to the hotel, praying that he hadn't made a mistake by giving Alicia a ring and accepting a signet band from her.

It was too late now. What was done was done. Still, every time he glanced at his hand or at hers, he felt bound to her, as if they'd just exchanged silent vows.

But they hadn't, he reminded himself. He'd already told her that his gift was to be worn with no strings attached, and that included heartstrings.

They settled into their rooms, and later they got ready to head out again, to return to Suva to go clubbing.

He put on a white shirt, a black jacket and black trousers. Alicia zipped her curvaceous body into a slim-fitting dress. She wore smoky eyeliner and the Twilight Temptation lipstick, too.

"There's a blues club I figured we could go to," he

said. "It's supposed to be mellow, more of an older crowd. Some of the clubs in Suva can get pretty rowdy, and I'd just as soon avoid a trendy or dangerous scene."

She put the finishing touch on her outfit, slipping on a pair of strappy heels. "Me, too."

He checked out her shapely legs and imagined them wrapped hotly around him. "We need to get some condoms for later. We're out."

She turned to look at him. "We are?"

"We used the last one last night." And he intended to make love with her tonight, as many times as his body would allow. He crossed the room to kiss her, and when they were locked in a deep embrace, he didn't want to release her. But he had to. He wasn't going to keep Alicia.

He stepped back. "Are you ready to go?"

She nodded. "Are you?"

"Yes." He was ready to make this their final night, while he did his damnedest not to fall in love.

Griffin and Alicia left the hotel. But he didn't forget the condoms. He bought some at a pharmacy on the way to the club and crammed them in the glove box of the rental car.

Sex wasn't love. He could be with Alicia without loving her. Or he hoped to God he could. He was terrified that he was on the verge of losing what was left of his screwed-up heart.

He hadn't thought it possible to be in this position within the span of two weeks, but here he was, fighting his feelings.

He parked the car, and Alicia smiled at him. She was beaming. But why wouldn't she be? She was ignoring his "no strings" warning. He could see the hope in her eyes, and that scared him most of all.

The club was dark, the décor woodsy. A live band played soul-stirring blues, setting the mood. Mature Fijians and well-behaved tourists sat in close-knit booths, eating dinner, sipping cocktails and bobbing their heads. A handful of couples danced, swaying to a cover version of "Down in the Alley," an old Memphis Minnie song about prostitution being performed in an alley.

Griffin and Alicia ordered grilled steaks and mint juleps, inspired by the next cover tune, "One Mint Julep." The drinks were Alicia's idea. She'd never had a mint julep. But neither had Griffin.

She clanked her glass against his and whispered, "To the condoms you bought."

Well, hell, he thought. That was as good a toast as any. Especially since it reminded him of how badly he wanted to be inside her tonight.

After they sipped their juleps, he leaned in to kiss Alicia, and they Frenched at the table, something Griffin wasn't normally prone to do. But he couldn't seem to stop himself.

"You taste like mint and bourbon," she said.

"And sugar and water? So do you." But those were the ingredients in their drinks.

"It's sexy," she mused.

"Yeah, it is." He went for another kiss, indulging once again.

She seemed to want more of him, too. Icy wet, their tongues mated. If Griffin didn't slow down, he was going to have the king of hard-ons. But before things went that far, he pulled back.

Soon their meals were delivered and they ate steak and potatoes. They skipped dessert and decided to dance.

The bluesy pulse of the music and the warmth of her body so close to his nearly did him in. But he refrained from kissing her again, even if it consumed his mind.

Once the evening ended and they got in the car, he reached for her, and they necked like a couple of lust-crazed teenagers.

"Let's go to a deserted place," Alicia said. "Where no one can see us."

His zipper all but sparked. "You want to do it in the car?" Apparently she wasn't worried about the killer. But neither was he. They weren't on the beach, and he'd make sure that the doors were locked and they were safe and secure.

She gave him a siren's smile. "Why not? We've got protection with us."

The Trojans they'd toasted, he thought. "You don't have to ask me twice." He turned the key and started the engine.

He drove until he found a secluded spot, surrounded by foliage and bathed in moonlight. He hit the door locks.

"This is perfect," she said, removing the condoms from the glove box and handing him one.

He set it on top of the dashboard. Then he took off his jacket, put his forearm in the center console and undid his trousers.

Alicia went one better. She removed her panties, hiked up her dress and climbed in his lap.

He pushed the seat all the way back, and while she straddled him, they kissed. The foreplay was amazing, hot and hammering.

She went vampire, loosening his collar and giving him one of her deep-sucking hickeys. He welcomed the girl-to-guy branding, the stimulation only Alicia could provide. When she reached between their bodies and stroked him, he dropped his head back even farther. Her hand on his penis. Her mouth on his neck. How good could it feel?

Desperately good, he thought.

He used his fingers on her, rubbing, caressing, making her wet. A throaty sound escaped her lips.

The windows fogged accordingly, and he gazed through the mist. She rocked back and forth against his hand, and he worked her into a climax.

She lost focus and stopped stroking him, but it was better that way. If she kept milking him, he would lose it, too, and he wanted to come inside her.

Once her spasms subsided, she sat upright, and he looked directly at her. Her nipples pebbled beneath her dress, and her wild gypsy hair tumbled forward.

Griffin reached past her and snagged the condom off of the dashboard. He couldn't wait any longer. Like a man possessed, he tore into the packet.

Alicia watched him roll on the protection. As soon as it was fitted to his body, she bunched her dress above her hips, got into position and sank down on top of him.

He cupped her face and drew her closer so they could kiss. Then he circled her waist and lifted her up and down, encouraging her to ride him.

She moved with feminine fury, and he gripped her tighter. He could feel the griffin inside him, the beast clawing its way out.

Between the two of them, there was very little finesse

and only a semblance of grace. But they were too ravenous to care. Behind the wheel of a car wasn't the easiest place to make love. The space was confined, the leather seats slippery. But they weren't about to let it stop them from having the best damn sex of their lives.

The bunched portion of her dress slipped down, and she grabbed it and raised it up again, tying it into a knot so it would stay put. He was glad she did. He liked looking at her while their bodies were joined. He wanted to see as much of Alicia as he could.

"Do other people attack each other this way?" she asked.

"The horny ones do," he teased, pulling her toward him and devouring her luscious mouth.

They kissed so hard, teeth clanked and jaws rattled. If they'd gotten any rougher, they would've drawn blood.

She fought for a breath in between. But damned if she didn't come back for more.

He fed her craving, sparring with her tongue and bumping her tender lips. She impaled herself faster and deeper. He felt like a thrill seeker on a runaway roller coaster. He didn't want the ride to end. He wanted more chills, more naughty spills. She was so wet and warm and creamy, he tightened his gluts and thrust his hips, taking all there was to take.

She gasped, then shuddered in climax. He wondered if it was from the war-torn kissing. Or maybe it was because he'd slipped his hand between her legs and was rubbing her the way he'd done before. He knew how she liked it.

But she knew what he liked, too. She shimmied all over him, moving up and down while she came. He went crazy and thrust again, sliding fully inside her, and as his orgasm exploded, as it ignited every sizzling cell in his wracking body, his vision blurred, making Alicia look veiled and dusky.

Like one of the ghosts she claimed to have seen in his eyes.

In the seconds that followed, she collapsed on top of him with her face nestled against his hickey-grazed neck. He wrapped his arms around her, and his chest went horribly tight, a reminder that this was the beginning of the end. Come hell or high water, tomorrow he was driving her to the airport and putting her on a plane.

In the morning, Alicia battled a canyon-size hole in her heart. Griffin didn't stop her from packing her bags. He didn't profess his love. He didn't propose.

She glanced at the ring he'd given her and noticed how genuinely it sparkled. But the shiny stones provided little comfort. The ring had become a token of an affair that was dying.

After she and Griffin had messed around in the car last night, they'd returned to the hotel and made love two more times. But as morning rolled around, he'd started drifting further and further away from her, until he'd put an awkward distance between them.

"Are you hungry?" he asked. "We can have breakfast in the diner before we head out." He glanced at his watch. "We've got a little time."

Food was the last thing on her mind. "I don't think my stomach could handle a meal right now."

"Me, neither. But I thought I should offer, just in case you…"

He didn't finish what he was saying. Suddenly he looked as if he wanted to bridge the gap he'd created, as if he were going to reach out and take her in his arms and never let go.

But he didn't. He picked up his holster instead, arming himself for the day. Was he arming his emotions, too?

Alicia should have known better than to put her faith in hope, in love, in happily ever after. After she'd gotten burned by Jimmy, she should have learned her lesson and stayed off the second-chances track.

"I'm going to remain single," she said, struggling to get her independence back. "I'm not going to get married again."

"Yes, you are. Someday you'll—"

"No," she snapped. "I'm not." The man she loved was a few feet away, ripping her future to shreds. "Mr. Right doesn't exist."

He didn't respond. He didn't do anything. He just stood there, in his government suit and gun, looking big and broad and troubled.

Finally he said, "I'm sorry, Alicia. The last thing I ever wanted to do was hurt you. I just want what's best for you."

Her voice remained clipped. "Two weeks of sharing my bed doesn't make you an authority on what's best for me."

"No, but it makes me care about what happens to you. It makes me champion your happiness."

Before her eyes watered, she turned away and fussed with the luggage tags on her suitcases. If he wanted to be the champion of her happiness, all he had to do was ask her to be part of his life. But he hadn't even suggested that they keep in touch, no phone calls, no e-mails, no snail-mail letters, no communication whatsoever.

His cell phone rang, cutting into the quiet. She assumed it was Shauna, but as soon as he answered the call, she could tell it was Inoke and not his daughter.

"What's up?" he asked, then fell silent in the exchange. After listening to whatever the inspector was saying, he responded with, "Oh, hell. Read it to me."

Alicia turned to look at him. Something was going on with the case. She studied Griffin's grim expression as Inoke recited unidentifiable words into the phone. Alicia couldn't hear what was being said.

Griffin listened, then said into the receiver, "I'll be there as soon as I can. But I have to take Alicia to the airport first."

He hung up, put his phone away and ran a jerky hand through his hair. "A letter arrived. This time it was sent to the station. It was addressed to me."

Her heartbeat blasted her chest. "From the killer?"

"Yes. He claimed that he slashed another couple, but instead of leaving them where he killed them, he transported their bodies to another location and buried them. He's baiting me to find them."

"How is that possible? Where are you supposed to look?"

"He cited the general vicinity they're in. But it's a wooded area, so they could be buried anywhere. Inoke is already on his way with a crew of cops and a forensic team."

"The killer changed his MO."

"So it seems. But it could also be a hoax, a way to trick the profiler into digging around in the dirt for bodies that don't exist."

"And it could be real. You should go. Now. There's no reason for you to drive me to the airport. I can take a cab."

He gave her an incredulous look. "I'm not putting you in a taxi. I'm not sending you off alone."

"I won't be alone. The driver will be there." She smoothed her summer blouse, trying to appear more in control than she felt. "I'll ask hotel security to recommend a driver. They know all of the cabbies. I'll be fine, Griffin. Besides…"

"Besides…what?"

"I think it would be better if we skipped the airport scene. We don't need to say a big, dramatic goodbye." It would hurt too much, she thought. And she feared the setting might make her cry. It was too *Casablanca,* too Rick and Ilsa. "I'd rather go our own ways from here."

"It doesn't feel right. Letting you drive away like that."

She implored him with her gaze. "Then ask me to stay."

He made a pained expression. "I wish I could, but…" He hesitated, then said, "I can't. I just can't."

"Then you don't have a choice in the matter of how I leave this hotel." She fought to keep her voice from breaking. "Just go to your killer, and leave me be."

"He isn't *my* killer."

"Yes, he is. You've been inside his mind. You know him better than anyone." She headed for the phone on the nightstand and picked it up.

"What are you doing?" he asked.

"Calling security and arranging my transportation."

"I'll do it." He took the phone out of her hand and made the call. Afterward, he insisted on escorting her to the lobby and carrying her bags.

She would've preferred a bellhop, but she got the G-man who was jilting her instead.

Griffin walked her to the taxi, and the handpicked cabbie, a friendly old Fijian, loaded her bags in the trunk and returned to the driver's seat, giving them time alone.

"So this is it," Alicia said, standing on the curb.

"Yes, this is it," Griffin parroted.

She could tell that he wanted to kiss her, but he seemed concerned about overstepping his bounds or causing an emotional episode. So he didn't do it. He didn't even give her a hug.

It was all she could do not to embrace him, not to hold him for all eternity. Or cry like a baby in his arms. But like him, she maintained her public composure.

They said a softly spoken goodbye, and Alicia climbed in the backseat of the car. Griffin closed the door and flattened his palm against the window. When he moved away from the vehicle, his handprint remained.

The cabbie pulled away from the curb, and Alicia gazed at her lover, her *ex*-lover, through the glass. He didn't wave. He didn't move at all. He looked like a statue, except for the light breeze that stirred his hair.

She kept watching him, and he kept watching her. Until the car turned onto the road and they couldn't see each other anymore.

Griffin drove to the designated spot and met up with Inoke. The search was underway with cadaver-sniffing dogs in tow, but so far nothing had been found.

The forest foliage was dense, the ground riddled with leaves and gnarled roots.

"You made good time," the inspector said to him.

"I didn't drive Alicia to the airport. She preferred to take a cab."

When the other man spoke, his neatly trimmed moustache twitched. "You look troubled by her leaving."

He was. He felt downright sick inside. "I don't want to talk about it."

"Are you sure? I'm a good listener."

"I'm sure." How many years of studying human behavior did it take to analyze his own feelings, to accept the fact that he was fighting a losing battle? Too many, Griffin thought. He couldn't have handled this any worse if he'd tried.

But Alicia was better off without him.

Wasn't she?

Hours passed, and Griffin tried to concentrate on his job, but he couldn't get himself together.

"Earth to FBI," Inoke said.

Griffin turned to look at the other man. They were trudging through the terrain with the rest of the team, only Griffin was a million miles away.

"You're thinking about her," Inoke said.

"I'm trying not to."

"Maybe you better admit that you can't—" the inspector made an openhanded gesture "—live without her." He closed his hands and clasped them together. "My wife says that I wouldn't be able to live without her." He shrugged a little. "But what do wives know?"

A lot, Griffin thought. And this conversation was making him feel worse. "I shouldn't have let her go. I shouldn't have done it."

"So fix it. Call her. Tell her that you're a big, bad, woman-whipped agent." Inoke blew out a heavy sigh.

"Then get your rear in gear and focus on what's going on here."

Griffin made an excuse. "I won't be able to reach her. She's on the plane by now."

"So leave a message on her cell. She'll get it after she lands, and you two can patch things up from there." When Griffin frowned, Inoke asked, "What's the matter? You never spilled your guts in a voice mail?"

It wasn't voice mail that freaked him out. It was the spilling his guts part.

"All you have to say is 'I love you,'" Inoke told him. "Nothing more. Nothing less."

Was that true? Would it be enough? Or was he obligated to tell her about Katie, too? To admit the secret he'd been keeping? Yes, he was. He owed her the truth. But that could come later. For now, he just needed to tell her that he loved her. Because he did, God help him, he did.

"You're right," he said to the inspector.

"I always am." In spite of the seriousness surrounding them, the cop-in-charge grinned. "Now go make your call."

Griffin walked away for some privacy and prepared to speed-dial the number. But his phone chimed instead, signaling a text message.

He glanced at the display. It was Alicia's number. Was she still in Fiji? Had her flight been delayed?

Anxious, he pressed "view" to see the message.

And the script nearly knocked him to his knees.

I kidnapped her, Agent Malone. The witness you went to all that trouble to protect. I have her.

That was it, the full message, the taunting words that stayed on the screen.

With his heart in his stomach, Griffin spun around to alert Inoke. While they were standing in the middle of a forest looking for bodies that didn't exist, the woman Griffin loved was in the hands of a killer.

Chapter 14

No sounds emerged.

Alicia was trapped within eerie silence. She was bound and gagged and blindfolded, and she had no idea where she was.

It felt like the bowels of hell, as dark and deep as Satan's dungeon. The air was warm and stifling, and she was propped on the ground, leaning against a distorted wall.

She shuddered, and beneath the blindfold, tears burned her eyes. The back of her head throbbed, a dull, pounding ache. Was her scalp sticky with blood?

The man in the helmet had hit her with a blunt object and knocked her out. The way he'd hit the cab driver.

The kidnapping played in her mind, like a movie she couldn't escape.

They'd still been on an isolated road that led to the main highway when the driver had swerved to avoid a motorcycle that had come from nowhere and cut out around him. But then the bike veered off into the dirt and crashed into some brush.

The driver stopped to help, and Alicia got out of the car with him. Her mistake. His mistake. The man on the motorcycle was faking his injuries. He lay there with his helmet shielding his face, moaning in distress.

As the driver leaned over him, preparing to call an ambulance, he reared up and hit the cabbie on the side of the head. The driver went down. Alicia screamed and turned to run, and Helmut Man gave chase.

Her heart pounded with the memory, with the fear. Within seconds, he was there, behind her…

A crushing blow…

Blinding pain…

When she'd regained consciousness, she was trussed up like the worst kind of hostage, and he was dragging her into this dungeon.

This nowhere land.

He'd shoved her down and grabbed the front of her blouse and torn a button from it. She'd felt it come off. She'd expected him to keep ripping at her clothes, but he hadn't.

After that, he'd left the dungeon, his booted footsteps retreating in echoing beats.

Was he going to come back? To torture her? To slit her throat?

Something skittered across one of her wrist-bound hands, and she gasped into the gag. She envisioned that it was a scorpion, but prayed it was a gecko.

She tried to think of something comforting, but the only image that came to mind was Griffin.

The man who'd given her a jeweled heart…and sent her away.

* * *

While immersed in the search for Alicia, Griffin asked God to keep her in His care. He even asked the sun to shine upon her. According to ancient beliefs in Katie's culture, the sun was ascribed the power of life and death, and as long as it kept its flaming eyes on someone, that person was safe. For now, the orange ball in the sky burned bright. Griffin prayed that it remained that way, and shifted his thoughts to Alicia's cab driver.

At the onset of the search, he'd been found in a ravine off the side of a country road. He was alive but unconscious, and now he was being tended to at a hospital. His taxi was gone, stolen by the offender and used to transport Alicia to wherever she'd been taken. A motorcycle was left at the scene, but it was a stolen vehicle, as well.

It wasn't much of a puzzle. The pieces fit together easily. The UNSUB had staged an accident, and after he'd delivered a single blow to the driver, he'd gone after Alicia. Blood was found at the scene that didn't belong to the driver. Griffin was sure it belonged to Alicia.

His Alicia. Hurt and bleeding.

Inoke trudged beside Griffin. They were in a cane field west of the location where Alicia had been abducted. This was where the offender had used Alicia's phone to text Griffin.

It was now the area being searched. The same dogs that had been sniffing for cadavers in the forest had been put to work here, along with a K-9 unit trained in tracking missing persons. But they hadn't found anything except the discarded phone, which was clean of prints. The offender was smart enough to wear gloves.

"Officer Molias is on her way," Inoke said. "She wants to speak with you."

Griffin gazed out at the field and the village that surrounded it. "I'll be here." Knee-deep in pain and guilt.

He'd agreed to let Alicia take a taxi. He'd endangered her the way he'd endangered Katie. Only this time, he should have seen it coming. He should've anticipated that this was what the offender had been planning. It was his job to second-guess the killer.

Alicia had asked him when they'd first met if profilers ever made mistakes. He'd admitted that sometimes they erred, but this error could cost Alicia her life.

If she wasn't dead already.

No, he thought. *No.* Don't go there.

Twenty minutes later, Officer Molias—Nalani— arrived. She showed up in street clothes. She wasn't on duty today, but she was here to join the search.

"Alicia called me to say goodbye," she told Griffin. "This morning, soon after she got in the cab. Before she was kidnapped."

He stopped, turned, looked at her. "We recovered her phone. We're aware of who she called and when. But I can only imagine what she said." He swallowed around the tightness in his throat. "How sad she must have been."

"She was trying to stay strong, to keep from crying. But I heard tears in her voice."

Griffin was capable of crying, too. If Alicia didn't survive the kidnapping, neither would he.

He would never forget the heart-wrenching moment of watching the taxi drive away. What had he been thinking? Letting her go like that?

"She loves you, Agent Malone."

"I love her, too. And I'm going to find her. If she isn't here…" He gestured to the cane field, to the village, to everything within view. "I'm going to figure out where that son of a bitch took her. One way or another, I'm going to find her."

The dungeon remained quiet. Even the creature that had crawled across Alicia's hand disappeared.

Suddenly she thought about Katie and the night she'd been killed. Was this how she'd felt, bound and gagged and crammed in a closet? Did she sense that she was going to die?

What would happen to Alicia's body if she died? Would Griffin find it?

Please, she thought. *Don't let it end that way. Not for me and not for him.* She didn't want Griffin's last memory of her to be the same image he had of Katie.

But Alicia didn't know if she was going live through this. Dizzy and weak and tired, she feared that the devil himself was slithering through her veins, luring her deeper into his lair, forcing her to embrace the darkness.

The sun continued to shine, and the search went nowhere. They didn't find Alicia, not in the cane field and not in the nearby village, and now Griffin was racking his brain to second-guess the UNSUB.

Still at the field with cops lingering at the location, he sat in his car, going over his profile of the offender. This time, he wasn't going to miss the clues. He was going to uncover information that would take him to Alicia.

A knock sounded on the driver-side window, and he glanced up. It was Nalani. He motioned her to go around the other side of the vehicle. She did, opening the door and sitting beside him in the passenger seat.

She turned to face him. "Can I ask you something?"

"Go ahead."

"Did he do this because you and Alicia were...?"

"Sleeping together? No." Griffin explained, "In the text message, the offender referred to her as 'the witness.' He would have called her my whore or some other degrading term if he knew we were lovers."

"He didn't take her to break your heart?"

"He did it as a game." And Griffin kept berating himself for not seeing it coming. "The profiler versus the killer."

"Do you think she's still alive?"

"Yes." He refused to believe otherwise, even though he was scared of being wrong, of making another mistake. "I'm going to find her. Not her body."

"Isn't that what happened with your wife? You found..."

As a lifeless image of Katie surfaced, he pushed it to the recesses of his mind. He couldn't think dead thoughts. Not now. Not while his lover was out there.

"I don't think the offender knows about my wife," he said. "And even if he does, he isn't equating her with Alicia."

"But you are."

He sucked in a breath. "I'm trying not to."

"I can only imagine how hard this is for you. I can hardly take it."

He didn't respond. Nalani wasn't talking to him as if they were an agent and a cop. She was getting emotional and behaving like a friend, and he couldn't handle her fear on top of his own.

* * *

Alicia was afraid, so terribly afraid.

Her mind fluttered back and forth, between Griffin the man and griffin the mythical beast. She could see their blue eyes, both sets of them, behind her own blindfolded eyes.

What was happening? Was she awake? Or was she asleep? She felt strange, as if she were lost in a dream.

Or dying.

Griffin glanced at his ring and shook away a chill, a feeling of death, of despair, of losing Alicia.

"Are you all right?" Nalani asked, then quickly added, "Sorry. Stupid question."

"I just need to figure out where she is." Then everything would be okay. He would have her back in his arms, back in his life.

Wouldn't he?

His cop companion went quiet, giving him time to focus, which he was more than determined to do. Alicia had said that he knew the killer better than anyone, and he did.

He pored over his notes, one by one, then turned to Nalani and used her as a sounding board, hitting upon a key point from the day.

"The offender baited me into searching for bodies that didn't exist," he said.

She sat up a little straighter. "As a ruse to get you away from Alicia."

"What if it was more than that? What if it's a clue?"

"The nonexistent bodies?"

"No. The part about burying them." Griffin's thoughts were moving faster now, gunning toward a probable theory. "What if he left Alicia in a place that would automatically become her grave if I didn't find her in time? Where she could be left to die on her own?" From dehydration, he thought. Or from the wound that had been inflicted. "A place associated with death? Or with burials?"

"Like a morgue? Or cemetery? Or crematorium?"

He considered her suggestions and shook his head. "I think he would go for something more pagan, more ritualistic."

"More ancient Fijian?"

"Yes." He snared her gaze, and she made a concentrating face. She knew her homeland far better than he did. And so did the offender.

"There are burial caves between Narocivo and Namalata, but that's across the water from here, and you have to arrange to see them with a guide."

"What about on this island? Are there any burial caves here?"

"No. There's a cave in Northern Viti Levu that has a stalactite shaped like a six-headed snake, but it's a tourist attraction. And so is the cannibal cave on the coast. But…"

He jumped on her hesitation. "But what?"

"I think there's a cannibal cave in the highlands that isn't open to the public. That's difficult to access and not good for a tour."

"Because it's small and dark and gravelike?"

She nodded, and Griffin's heart punched his chest. "Do you know exactly where it is?"

"No. Like I said, I think it's in the highlands. I never paid much attention to it."

"We need to find out." He jumped out of the car to signal Inoke, praying to God and to the sun and whoever else would listen that Alicia was there.

Griffin headed up the rescue team. He wanted to be the first person to enter the cave, to find Alicia, to hold her, to help her.

But he was steeped in fear, too. What if this wasn't the right location? Or what if he was too late? What if she was...

Dead.

The word crept through his blood like a shiver. Dusk had fallen, making the landscape look harsh and jagged. Nalani had been right. The cave was in the highlands, nestled against a hillside in an isolated spot. It wasn't listed in guidebooks or revered by locals.

Griffin understood why. To him, it looked like the gateway to hell. He crouched through the opening, wearing a hard hat with a hands-free light attached. He had another stainless steel flashlight clipped to his belt, along with his gun. A medic came through behind him, packed with emergency supplies.

"This way," Griffin said. The path led in one direction.

His pulse pounded with every step. The terrain beneath his feet curved, bumpy in spots, smooth in others. As he continued, the cave got narrower. He could hear the medic behind him.

"It's a tight squeeze," he said to the other man. And getting tighter by the minute.

"I'm hanging in there."

"So are the bats." Griffin's light sent them into a tunnel that was too small for humans.

He rounded a corner and nearly lost his footing. "Loose rocks," he called back.

"Thanks," came the reply.

Another claustrophobic corner and then he turned into a wider area and saw her...

Bound, gagged and blindfolded, she was laying on what appeared to be an ancient altar that had been used for cannibalistic rites.

She was completely motionless. Déjà vu flashed in his mind. Katie in the closet, soaked with blood.

No pulse. No warmth. No life.

"You okay up there?" the medic asked.

"I found her," he responded, his hands trembling, his heart clawing its way to his throat. He couldn't tell if she was breathing.

He rushed forward, the medic fast on his heels. Alicia was pale and gaunt, dirty and scratched, her hair matted with blood. The top button was missing from her blouse, taken by the offender. That caused him to tremble even more.

Griffin steadied his hand and checked for a pulse.

Thump. Thump. Thump.

She was alive.

Tears rimmed his eyes, and he said her name, letting her know she was safe and hoping she could hear him.

She stirred and shuddered in his arms, as if awakening from a deathly dream. She'd been asleep, not unconscious, which was a good sign.

He removed the gag and blindfold, and while he unbound her wrists, she looked up him through confused eyes, as if the dream hadn't quite ended, as if he weren't quite real.

Then, a moment later, she burst into racking sobs, and he knew she'd come fully awake. Griffin continued to hold her, to soothe her, to keep her close.

The medic moved forward to assess her injuries, and soon Alicia was on her way to the nearest hospital.

Later that night, Griffin sat in a chair next to Alicia's hospital bed, a low light burning.

"Lie here with me," she said.

"Are you sure? I don't want to disturb you."

"Please." She held out a hand to him.

He accepted her invitation, getting into bed carefully and tucking the blanket around both of them. She'd suffered a concussion. She'd gotten stitches in her head, too.

"How long do you think they'll keep me here?" she asked.

"The doctor said it would probably be a couple of days." He breathed in the soap and antiseptic scent of her. To him, it was the most beautiful fragrance in the world. "I love you, Alicia."

She turned in his arms, and he absorbed the pain of who she was, of what had happened to her.

"Don't say that just because I got hurt," she told him. "Don't say it unless you mean it."

"I do mean it. I loved you when I let you go. I'd been fighting it, but it was there, deep inside. Then Inoke drew it out of me."

Her sleepy eyes went wide. "Really?"

Griffin nodded. "I was getting ready to call you when the offender sent me a text and told me that he'd kidnapped you." He pressed a light kiss to her brow, but inside he was still trembling, much like the moment when he'd found her in the cave. The fear of losing her hadn't gone away. "I want to propose, to ask you to share my life, but I'm afraid that you won't remember this conversation in the morning. Or even weeks from now. Sometimes brain injury patients forget—"

"I won't. Ask me." She gazed at him, the dusky light making her look even more vulnerable. "Ask me."

His heart banged against his chest. He was nervous. Excited. Breathless. But being in love did that to a man. "Will you marry me?" he asked, keeping the question simple.

"Yes." She kept her answer just as simple. "I'd be honored to be your wife. I love you, too. And I always will."

Would she?

He touched her cheek, and she snuggled closer, her sleepy eyes fluttering closed. As soon as she was well, he would tell her about Katie and pray that it wouldn't destroy what she felt for him.

Every time Alicia looked at Griffin she wanted to cry. Good tears. Emotional tears. He sat on the edge of her bed, looking at her, too.

He'd remained with her for every second of her hospital stay, and this afternoon, she was being released as soon as the paperwork was complete.

She hadn't forgotten a thing, least of all his marriage proposal. She was going to remember every word he'd spoken, along with every gentle touch.

Still, something didn't feel right. Not with her, but

with him. He seemed worried, as if something weighed on his mind.

"What's wrong?" She paused, held her breath. "Did the cab driver die?"

"No. He should come out of this all right."

The cabbie's head injury had been much more severe than hers. The last she'd heard he was in critical condition. "So, he's stable now?"

"Yes. He's getting better."

"Then what is it? What's wrong?"

"It's about Katie." His chest heaved. "You're the only person I've told this to, and I wish I didn't have to say it, but I do."

Alicia waited, fearful of what his next words would be.

He said, "She didn't have to die that weekend. If I'd stayed home…"

"You're blaming yourself? That's what this is about? Oh, Griffin, you—"

"No, you don't understand. She asked me to stay home. She was lonely, and she wanted to be with me. But I put her off. I promised her that we'd take a romantic vacation as soon as I got a break in my schedule."

She searched his eyes and saw remnants of the ghosts. "It still isn't your fault."

"I was always doing that to her. Making promises I didn't keep. I loved her. So help me, I did. But I took advantage of her giving nature. I wasn't as good a husband as I could have been. *Should* have been," he amended.

"I thought about her when I was in the cave. I didn't want you to find my body the way you'd found hers."

"I would have gone crazy if that happened. I would have lost it for sure."

Alicia gestured to the ring on his finger. "Don't forget, that's from Katie, too. I think we found a griffin in Fiji because she wanted us to find it. She isn't blaming you for what happened to her, and she doesn't want you to blame yourself, either."

"I hope you're right."

"I am. I know I am. If I were Katie, that's what I'd want. For you to go on with your life and be happy."

The haunting in his eyes seemed paler, less painful. "I was worried that this would change how you feel about me."

"It doesn't. Not a bit. I still love you." She would marry him this very instant if she could.

"Thank you," he said, his voice humbled. "I love you, too. And so will my daughter. She's going to be thrilled about the brothers and sisters we're going to give her."

Ah, yes, Alicia thought. Babies. "How many can I have?"

"As many as you want." He crawled across the bed to kiss her, and the taste of him filled her heart.

When the kiss ended, they gazed quietly at each other. But outside of the hospital, things weren't quite so silent. Reporters clamored for a story, hoping to interview Alicia's family and friends.

But no one had come to visit. Griffin had called everyone, including Zoë and Madeline, and asked them to keep a cautious distance, guarding them from the press. Naturally, security measures had been taken to protect Alicia. A uniformed officer was stationed at her door.

"What's going to happen now?" she asked.

"With what?"

"The press. Are you going to sneak me out of here when I'm released?"

"Yes," he reassured her. "I've got a plan in place."

"What about the—" she took a deep, shaky breath "—killer?"

"He already made contact."

A chill zigzagged across her spine. "He did? How?"

"He sent another letter to the station addressed to me. It arrived this morning. Inoke e-mailed an encrypted copy to my laptop." Which Griffin had with him at the hospital. "I read it while you were sleeping. It said, 'Good game, Agent Malone. Now I can have some fun elsewhere.'"

"Fun?" Her chills deepened.

"Looking for more couples to kill. You and I were just a little fancy on the side. But he's done with us."

"How can you be sure?"

"He returned the button from your blouse. It was inside the letter. If I'd lost the game, if you'd died, he would have kept it."

She'd discovered, the hard way, that buttons were the tokens the killer took from his victims. "So I don't matter to him anymore."

"Neither do I. Not the way I did. Especially since I'm leaving the Pacific, too."

Alicia nodded. Griffin was taking her home to Virginia, where they could be together and he could work from the States. He would still be immersed in the Sex on the Beach Killer case, but he would be consulting the Fijian police through phone calls and e-mails. He was certain that the offender was going to get caught, particularly now that he and his team had created such an in-depth profile on him. It was just a matter of when and where.

And by whom, Alicia thought.

Griffin reached for her again, holding her close. "I won't let you down. I'm going to be the best husband I can be."

"I know you will."

"When you were lost from me, I asked God and the sun to keep you safe."

"I understand about God. But the sun?"

While he explained the Choctaw story, she listened to him—the man who'd saved her, who'd rescued her from darkness.

And now, as daylight streamed through the window and bathed them in a golden glow, she thanked God and the sun that she was where she belonged.

Safe and warm, she thought, with Special Agent Griffin Malone. For the rest of her life.

* * * * *

Griffin's job is done and he and Alicia can plan their future. But the killer is still out there…as one more Secret Traveller is about to find out.

Don't miss the super-sexy, super-thrilling conclusion to SEDUCTION SUMMER, Killer Affair *by Cindy Dees. Available August 2009 only from Mills & Boon® Intrigue.*

0709/46a

INTRIGUE

Coming next month

2-IN-1 ANTHOLOGY

COLTON'S SECRET SERVICE by Marie Ferrarella

Undercover agent Nick needs to concentrate on protecting a senator. Yet beautiful distraction Georgie Colton has other things in mind!

RANCHER'S REDEMPTION by Beth Cornelison

Thrown into the path of danger, red-hot rancher Clay must work with his ex-wife to uncover secrets about a crime as well as their true feelings for each other.

2-IN-1 ANTHOLOGY

THE HEART OF BRODY McQUADE by Mallory Kane

People said that no woman would find her way into tall, dark cop Brody McQuade's heart. Could Victoria prove them wrong?

KILLER AFFAIR by Cindy Dees

When Maddie and Tom's plane crashes on a remote island they're suddenly at the mercy of a killer. Can rugged Tom keep Maddie alive *and* win her heart?

SINGLE TITLE

DARK LIES by Vivi Anna
Nocturne

The last thing werewolf Jace wants to do is partner up with human police escort Tala. But she has a dark secret that could bind them together forever...

On sale 17th July 2009

Available at WHSmith, Tesco, ASDA, Eason and all good bookshops.
For full Mills & Boon range including eBooks visit
www.millsandboon.co.uk

® ™ INTRIGUE

Coming next month

2-IN-1 ANTHOLOGY

SHEIKH PROTECTOR by Dana Marton

Karim was the most honourable sheikh and fiercest warrior throughout the kingdom. He vowed to protect Julia and her unborn child, but he didn't bank on falling in love!

SCIONS: REVELATION by Patrice Michelle

Nocturne

When Emma's aunt is captured, she must join forces with mysterious yet sexy Caine to set the worlds of the vampires, werewolves and panthers on their true paths.

SINGLE TITLE

LOADED by Joanna Wayne

Oil tycoon Matt Collingsworth couldn't abide his name being dragged through the mud. But for determined CIA agent Shelley he was willing to get dirty!

SINGLE TITLE

BODYGUARD TO THE BRIDE by Dani Sinclair

Posing as Zoe's bodyguard was Xavier's most challenging mission yet. And once he got his hands on the pregnant bride it would be impossible to give her away!

On sale 7th August 2009

2 FREE

BOOKS AND A SURPRISE GIFT!

We would like to take this opportunity to thank you for reading this Mills & Boon® book by offering you the chance to take TWO more specially selected titles from the Intrigue series absolutely FREE! We're also making this offer to introduce you to the benefits of the Mills & Boon® Book Club™—

- ★ FREE home delivery
- ★ FREE gifts and competitions
- ★ FREE monthly Newsletter
- ★ Exclusive Mills & Boon Book Club offers
- ★ Books available before they're in the shops

Accepting these FREE books and gift places you under no obligation to buy, you may cancel at any time, even after receiving your free shipment. Simply complete your details below and return the entire page to the address below. You don't even need a stamp!

YES! Please send me 2 free Intrigue books and a surprise gift. I understand that unless you hear from me, I will receive 4 superb new titles every month for just £3.19 each, postage and packing free. I am under no obligation to purchase any books and may cancel my subscription at any time. The free books and gift will be mine to keep in any case.

19ZED

Ms/Mrs/Miss/Mr ....Initials ....
BLOCK CAPITALS PLEASE

Surname ....

Address ....

....

....Postcode.............................

Send this whole page to:
UK: FREEPOST CN81, Croydon, CR9 3WZ